Evernight Publishing

www.evernightpublishing.com

Editor: Karyn White

Cover Artist: Sour Cherry Designs

ISBN: 978-1-77233-179-0

MURPHY

DEDICATION

I would like to say a big thank you to Evernight for giving The Skulls a home. Without them Murphy wouldn't be here now. Also, a huge thank you to my readers. I hope you love Murphy and Tate as much as I do.

MURPHY

MURPHY

The Skulls, 2

Sam Crescent

Prologue

Tate, age sixteen

"So you're the poor schmuck that has been forced to babysit me?" Tate asked. She liked the guy in front of her. His leather jacket marked the label of prospect whereas everything else about him was completely strong. Forcing herself not to admire his body, Tate left the door and walked toward the kitchen. The scent of homemade lasagna filled the air.

"I've got a name."

She turned to see the prospect leaning against the door. His hair was down to his neck, and his muscles were so thick, she was surprised he even fit into the leather cut jacket. He was tall. Would he make Tiny look small?

"What is it?" she asked, grabbing a glass from a cupboard. Eva had some errands to run and wouldn't be home 'til late. Part of her hoped her nanny had a date. Her father, Tiny, refused to give Eva the time of day, but Tate knew he had feelings for the other woman.

"The name's Murphy." His arms folded over his large chest, and she couldn't help but wonder how it would feel to have his arms wrapped around her.

Sixteen, Tate, not going to happen.

"I'm Tate." She poured some milk into her glass, staring at him over the rim as she took a sip. "Do you want some?" He snorted, and she couldn't help but roll her eyes. "One glass of milk is not going to turn you into a pussy. I won't see you any differently, Murphy."

Ignoring his bewildered look, she poured him a glass. She left him in the kitchen and headed toward the sitting room where the latest horror movie was playing. Tate turned the movie on.

Murphy walked into the room, and he was staring at her. Glancing toward him, she saw his head was cocked to the side as he looked at her.

"What?"

"You're not going to get all bitchy and cause me problems?" He took a seat opposite her. She quickly paused her movie and focused on the rough biker in front of her.

"It's Friday night. Shouldn't you be at a party?" she asked.

"My duty is here."

"Yeah, I bet it's going to be a blast." Sitting back, she smiled at him. "You better get ready for a riot, Murphy. I've got a party planned. My friends from school are coming to tear this house to shit. You'll be wishing for something different by then." It took every ounce of willpower inside herself not to laugh.

He looked panicked. "You are going to be difficult." Murphy stood looking ready to cause havoc.

Laughing, Tate shook her head. "I'm not having a party. My plans consist of watching this horror movie then a chick flick. I'll also be eating lasagna that Eva made, but—hold it—I might go all out and drizzle some hot sauce over it." She wasn't in the mood to party tonight. Eva asked her not to cause too many waves as Tiny was going through something at the club.

He started laughing, and Tate knew she had him. "I'm not a bitch, and I'm not going to be causing you trouble, at least not tonight. We've got other nights for that."

After some minutes passed he finally sat back. Tate felt his eyes on her at all times. What was he thinking? She didn't understand what was going on. Her body was all over the place. Tate felt her nipples tighten and heat flood her core. She'd never felt anything like this. None of the guys in high school appealed to her. They bullied her whenever she was alone. Sure, she went to parties because she did have some friends, but tonight she hadn't been in the mood to be putting on a show.

"Why are you not at a party or something?" Murphy asked.

"I'm not exactly the most popular girl in school." She kept her gaze on the movie, which she'd pressed play to. Tate was popular at school but for all the wrong reasons. The guys were only interested in getting in with The Skulls while the girls wanted an in for the members.

"Why not? You're beautiful, and your father is the leader of one of the toughest motorcycle gangs known in this area."

She felt aglow at the fact he thought she was beautiful. He was the first man, besides her father, who thought she was beautiful. Tiny didn't count in the scheme of things. All fathers were supposed to think their daughters were beautiful.

"It doesn't exactly help matters. I'm happy on my own." She smiled at him not wanting to get into it. The parties she went to were to help with the boredom. Also, Tiny wouldn't let her go to any of the club parties.

He didn't make another comment and didn't complain as she put in another movie, this time a romance. When her stomach started to growl, she offered him some food and grabbed them both some.

By the time the movie ended, Murphy was sat on the sofa with her. His arm was across the back of the sofa, and for a few seconds she could imagine him as her boyfriend. He didn't creep her out at all.

"It's time for bed," she said, getting up and yawning. "I'll see you tomorrow?"

"You sure will."

She smiled. "You really did get the rough end of the stick."

Murphy shook his head. "No, I got the best part of the deal. Have a nice night, Tate."

Watching him take a seat, she turned away and went toward her bedroom. Her heart was pounding, and she wondered how she was going to act nonchalant around him. Murphy was completely different from many of the prospects sent to guard her.

None of them liked babysitting duty. She was never a bitch or hard work to them unless you counted the occasional party she attended. Tate knew they were doing duties in order to become a Skull. Most of them hated being around her though. She put it down to them hating how boring she was. Shrugging, she quickly got ready for bed and tried to blank out Murphy's presence in her house.

The following Friday Murphy carried her out of the latest party she'd been invited to. She loved the feel of his arms around her. When he got her home, he held her head down the toilet as she spewed everything up.

"I didn't mean to be difficult," she said, groaning.

"Honey, this is nothing to what I've seen."

****

Tate, age seventeen

"Men are annoying," Tate said, throwing a stone out across the lake. Murphy was sat on his bike watching her. After class she'd walked all the way to the lake, which was located a few miles out of town. She didn't mind the walk. It helped her to get over the heartache of another rejection. Murphy had offered her relationship advice and told her to get out there. *Big mistake*. The only guy she enjoyed spending time with was sat astride his bike. He was close to being patched in.

He deserved a spot in The Skulls. Murphy was loyal, and he'd never once blabbed to her father about the parties she attended.

Her father had told her Murphy offered to take care of her. She knew her father liked the thought of Murphy looking after her rather than a prospect. Once the man before her got patched in, he was a Skull.

"I take it Ben was not very welcoming of your attentions?" Murphy asked, folding his arms.

"No, he sucks like everyone else."

She watched him climb off his bike and come toward her. He wrapped his arms around her, and she sank against him. The scent of leather and his own natural smell overwhelmed her. She wanted to soak everything up about him.

"Hey," he said, lifting her head up by a finger under her chin. "If he can't see how amazing you are then the bastard is not worth it." He pressed a hand to her chest, above her breast. Tate almost swallowed her own tongue. "No man is worth your kindness if they can't show it back."

"You told me to get out there."

"I lied. Don't become something you don't want to be. There's nothing wrong with you. Besides, you sure know how to party, and if he can't appreciate that, then fuck him."

She sighed, stepping back. Tate had to create space between them before she did something she would regret. "You don't think there's anything wrong with me?"

"Nah. The only thing I'd change is how damn sweet you are. Someone is going to destroy that part of you, Tate, and I'd hate to see that happen." He leaned down and brushed his lips against her cheeks.

Her stomach tightened as she tensed. The small touch made the hairs on her arm stand on end.

"Now, get your ass on my bike. I've got popcorn waiting. I'm not letting you out of my sight tonight."

Murphy dropped her off at home to finish preparations for their movie night. He left her for an hour, and when he returned his knuckles were bruised. She didn't give it much thought until she saw Ben at school the following week. Whoever dated Ben for the next couple of weeks was not going to get the picture perfect guy.

Seeing the bruises should have bothered her. Tate couldn't help but smile, knowing Murphy had seen to the guy who hurt her. She made a promise to herself that the parties were going to stop. There was nothing gracious or graceful about a woman vomiting down a toilet from too much alcohol.

****

Tate, age eighteen

Murphy had danced with her all night. His arms wrapped around her with his scent surrounding her as they moved together. She was so totally in love with him. He was more than her babysitter or friend. When he'd been patched in she'd been so happy for him. She hadn't been invited to the party, but he'd come to visit her at home. Eva turned a blind eye to his presence.

Even in drink, Murphy was adorable.

When no date had come to collect her, Murphy had decided she wasn't going to her prom alone. She'd been more than happy to go alone. He wouldn't have any of it, offering his arm as they went to the dance.

She ignored the whispers as people pointed her out. None of them knew her, and she wasn't going to let them spoil this one night that was all her own.

"Are you ready to get out of here?" he asked.

"Yeah, I'm ready."

Murphy escorted her out of the dance, and together they left the building. He didn't take her anywhere, and she smiled up at him. "School is almost finished."

"I know." He leaned against his bike, stroking her cheek. "You look so damn beautiful."

"I'm eighteen as well."

He tensed, and she wished she'd kept her mouth shut. "I know this is going to scare the living hell out of you, but I need to say it." She bounced on her feet, ignoring the pain from her heels. "I love you, Murphy. It doesn't make any sense, and you don't need to say anything to me, but I needed you to know how I feel."

She waited for him to curse or growl. He did neither.

His hand banded around her waist, tugging her close. "I could be fucking killed for the way I feel about you."

Tate gasped as his head lowered.

"I've told myself time and time again to leave you the fuck alone. You don't need me in your life. You're Tiny's daughter. You deserve so much more than me, but

I can't stay away. I love you too damn much." His lips claimed hers, making her moan. She gripped his arms, needing to get closer to him.

Murphy plundered her mouth, and she whimpered. Sensation was running riot throughout her whole body. His hands sank into her hair, holding her in place.

"We could go somewhere," Tate said.

"What?"

"It's prom night. I'm ready." She looked into his eyes to see the answering arousal reflected back at her.

"No, we're not doing this tonight." He ran his fingers over her lip. "We've got all the time in the world. Tonight we're going to have fun and celebrate."

He kissed her again. For the rest of the night she was on cloud nine. Murphy was attentive and spent the whole night telling her how much he loved her.

If she was in a dream she never wanted to wake up.

****

Murphy's betrayal

Tate stared across the space at the mall. Another prospect was with her, but she didn't care. Only a few weeks ago she'd been loving her life and wishing it would never end. It had all been a lie. Murphy had taken the piss out of her. She'd seen him with the women from The Lions. All the time she'd been with him, he'd been preparing to leave.

Her father was outraged by his betrayal. She was heartbroken by what he'd done. There were times she found herself crying from what he'd done.

Don't think about it or him.

Across the mall she saw him as if she'd thought him into being. His arm was slung around a blonde woman, and across the way she saw him fondling the woman's breast. A wave of sickness swept through her.

The pain suddenly peaked, and she didn't know what the hell to do. Then, as if a switch had gone off in her mind, she glared over at him. Grabbing her bag, she ignored the prospect walking with her, and she began shopping. Tiny had sent her out with his credit card. Eva had told him how she'd been heartbroken.

No more. She'd let herself love Murphy, and she refused to let another man close to her. Blanking the prospect she started shopping, and as the hours passed, she felt something shift inside her.

Murphy was gone and never coming back, but she didn't need to be broken. No man deserved to be given that much control. Gritting her teeth, she forced herself to not care. Stepping out of the shop she collided with the group of Lions. The men took a step back as the prospect pulled her behind him. She couldn't even remember the guy's name who'd been sent to babysit her.

Looking through the group she settled on Murphy. She couldn't read his gaze. Blocking him out, she turned to the guy she'd crashed into.

"Move," she said. Her voice was hard and unwavering. The one man she cared about, loved, was gone.

Never let another man inside.

"Who the fuck are you talking to?" the guy asked.

Glaring at him, she looked up and down his body.

"Scum." She shoved past the Lion and stormed away without looking back. Murphy was gone, and there was no way she was ever letting him near her again.

Be the bitch he thought you'd be.

Chapter One

One month from Lash

"Of all the fucked up shit I've had to deal with in the last few weeks this is the worst," Tiny said, yelling across the room. "My daughter won't speak to me, and now she's moved out of my home to live in town, alone."

Murphy listened to his leader, his president, curse Tate. He knew the anger as he was feeling the same. Tate refused to have anything to do with him or her father. Every member of the club had tried to draw her back into their world, but each time she cut them down short. The only time she'd talk to him was when he entered the dentist surgery where she worked. Holding in the chuckle, he wasn't about to admit to his brothers his new obsession, stalking Tate Johnson.

"Something funny, Murphy?" Tiny asked. The older man had a short temper at the best of times, but now, it was seriously short.

"Do you know where she's working?" Murphy kept his hands locked in front of him. He was surrounded by his brothers once again, and everything finally felt right in his world. For the past couple of years he'd been with another club, The Lions, to gain information for Tiny that would help his club. They were the longest years of Murphy's life. He'd seen things that he never wanted anyone to know. The Skulls were hard, rough bastards, but they had rules. The Lions never lived by any rules.

"She's a receptionist for a fucking dentist. Yeah, I know where my daughter's working." Tiny threw down the cell phone he'd been holding, and silence fell in the room. Glancing around Murphy saw Lash was looking at his watch while Nash bounced his leg up and down. Butch, Hardy, Zero, Mikey, and several other members were sat waiting for the next lot of business.

The first line of business was dealing with Tate. She'd been part of the club but was never allowed to stay over. Tiny was very protective of her and demanded the upmost respect for his only child.

"She'll come around," Lash said, interrupting the silence.

"Tate talking to Angel?"

"Yes."

Murphy tuned out trying to think of a better way to deal with Tate than force her back, caveman style.

"I'm sending Steven to keep an eye on her. He's healthy, but I want to make sure he's completely up to the job before we patch him in," Tiny said.

A couple of months ago two of their prospects, Steven and Blaine, had been shot and almost killed trying to protect their women. Their intended sacrifice and intervention had given them the patches they'd been waiting for. Murphy had a lot of respect for the two men, and he did believe they'd make a good addition to The Skulls.

"I want that job," Murphy said, looking at Tiny.

"Tate hates your guts," Nash said, speaking up for once.

"My job was to take care of her before, and I can do it again." Murphy ignored their stares. "I've got this. I fucked up, and I can fix it."

Tiny stared at him for several minutes. Everyone knew not to interrupt him when he was thinking. "Fine, you make it worse and I'm shooting you. Next order of business, some of The Lions want to patch in. Murphy, give us the lowdown on what's going on."

Sitting back, Murphy gave them the information on the three men waiting outside for a chance to patch in.

"They didn't like the old ways, but they put up with it because they didn't have anything else. The shit that went over there was rough."

"If they do drugs then I'm out," Hardy said.

"Shut up. Tell us about them." Tiny gave him the instruction.

Standing up, Murphy moved to the blind and lifted it up. The three men were too busy looking around the bar at the old ladies and sweet-butts to see them staring.

"The big guy, over six foot five, is Killer. He's a little like Lash and can kill with his bare hands. It doesn't scare him to use them on men who need it. The Lions got kicks out of him killing for sport. Underground fighting and all that shit was where they got shit-loads of money."

"Should we have someone like that on our team?" Butch asked.

"He's a good guy and refused to go to your house, Tiny." Murphy liked the guy and would do anything to get him in with The Skulls.

"Fine, we'll talk. Stop fucking interrupting, or I'll deal with this alone. The next one," Tiny said.

"Whizz, computer geek and hard ass. Don't let the glasses and skinny look fool you. He's a hard-nosed bastard and doesn't like to be crossed."

"How the fuck did you escape then?" Lash asked.

Murphy knew Lash and Nash were going to be hard on him. They'd grown up with Tate, considering her a sister they needed to protect.

"Everything I did was to help this fucking club. Don't give me shit about stuff you don't know about. The last one is Time. He was always on time for everything. The guy has a built in brain like clockwork."

He sat back in his seat waiting for more instructions.

"Bring them in," Tiny said.

Getting up, Murphy opened the door, whistling for the three men to come inside. Killer took the lead with the other two following close behind him. Murphy stood beside them. He noticed The Skulls grew tense at the sight of insignia on the leather jacket. Most of The Lions were gone, but the cut was still being worn.

"Murphy vouches for you, and that means something to me. One month probation and then we'll give you a chance to get patched. After the month you can then earn your place within the club. We'll decide when you become a member. It could take a week, a month, or years, but I get the final fucking say. If it doesn't work out in this month for you guys to be given a chance, then you're gone without a trace, get me?" Tiny asked.

All three men nodded.

"Good, give me your fucking jackets." Each of the three men handed over the leather jackets with hesitation. Murphy's own jacket he'd burned, along with every single reminder of his time within the other club.

"Burn this shit." Tiny threw the cuts at Hardy who then left to deal with it. "I don't know what shit went on back in your club, and I don't care. Here, now, you respect my rules. No drugs, it's not an option for me. We deliver them, but we don't use or deal them here in Fort Wills. If you're given a job, you do it without any questions asked. When a woman says no, it means no. Follow the rules, respect the club, respect the patch, and you'll learn the rest as you go."

Tiny slammed his hand down on the table. "Meeting finished. Get the fuck out of here. Murphy, I want a word with you."

He watched the others leave, nodding at Killer, Whizz, and Time to wait for him.

Lash was the last to leave, closing the door behind him.

"What's the matter?" Murphy asked.

"Tate hates you, and I know shit went down with the two of you before you left. What's going on?" Tiny stood up, looking every part the scary biker. He wasn't wearing his jacket, and it showed his thick, tattooed arms folded across his chest.

"She was in love with me, and there were feelings there. I broke her heart, but I did what I had to. I put the club first." Murphy kept his gaze on the older man. He expected Tiny to lose it very soon. "I'll always put the club first." It was hard to get the words out, but he knew what was expected of him. Murphy knew the moment he made that promise all those years ago to Tate.

Tiny nodded. "Patricia learned to deal with the club coming first. Her death was hard to deal with. I had this place to keep me going. I love my daughter. Don't make her promises you can't keep."

Murphy agreed letting himself out of the room. Several of the men were wrapped around the sweet-butts. Taking a seat near the bar he ordered a shot of whiskey. He needed to calm his nerves. For the past three months he'd been back in the fold of The Skulls. Some of his brothers were still apprehensive around him, Tiny included. Did they think he turned while he'd been away?

"Hey, baby, do you want some company?" Fern asked, sliding up against him. She was one of the worst sweet-butts in the club, fucking anyone who'd have her. He remembered her trying to get one of the members to marry her, but she was a sweet-butt and would always be a sweet-butt.

"It's not going to happen, Fern. Fuck off." Murphy pushed her away.

"Do you seriously have a hang up on that fat bitch?" Fern's voice rose. "Tate's not even around here, and the last thing you'll get is between those chubby thighs."

Her words about Tate pissed him off. Acting without thinking, he grabbed her around the throat and slammed her head against the bar. The contact wasn't harsh, but it had her gasping and shaking. "You ever talk about Tate like that again and I'll fucking kill you. You're a whore around here, Fern. No one wants you for anything other than a good hole. Tate is old lady material. You, you're not."

No one interfered as he grabbed his beer and walked outside. He noticed no one went running to Fern's defense. The old ladies hated her, and the men used her.

Going behind the club he stared out at the mass of trees located behind their building. He would stand out here many times when looking out for Tate. She was such a hard woman to understand when he took care of her. Tate hadn't been difficult or a bitch. She'd been this carefree spirit looking for a good time. Over the years he'd lost count of the parties he'd dragged her out of, but she'd never fought him when he removed her from the partying scene. He remembered the fact she simply stopped going to parties. Every time he did pull her out of a party he kept the information to himself and made sure Eva looked after her if she'd drunk too much.

Killer cleared his throat. Turning to look at him, Murphy saw the doubt on the other man's face.

"What's the matter?" Murphy asked.

"The men don't like me or the others. We're thinking of cutting and running," Killer said, surprising him. Murphy never had them tagged for quitters.

"You came from another group known for its lack of rules. If you want to quit, then quit, but don't make that decision lightly."

"Why?"

"Because you'll have a mark on your head like the rest of The Lions. Tiny wants you all dead, and he'll find each and every one of you." Murphy let his words settle between them. Reaching into the back of his pocket, he grabbed his pack of smokes and lit one up.

"I wasn't part of that shit," Killer said.

"Then prove it. Become a member and fight each and every one of them." Murphy offered the other man a smoke.

"Fight, again?"

Murphy shrugged. "You want to die? Then run. You don't want to die then you fight and prove to these men that you're worth the risk of having you in the club."

For several minutes he finished smoking his cigarette and threw the butt away. "I've got a woman to go and protect."

****

Tate left the dentist building where she worked. It was fucking boring, but it made her enough money to get by. The apartment wasn't too bad either. Several of the women, dental nurses, and fellow receptionists mumbled as she passed them. She was used to the name calling and ignored them. Only a couple of weeks had passed since she left her father's home, but she knew it was the best decision she'd made.

Grabbing her cell phone from her bag she saw several missed calls from Tiny, Lash, and Nash. She ignored them all, deleting any messages from the club. The Skulls was not her life. Her father would never let her become a member. Women were not allowed in the club, and the club always came first. She was tired of being second best.

Pocketing her phone she headed away from the group of the women.

"Tate?" One of the women called out to her, but she kept on walking. "Tate."

The sound of running feet had her stopping, turning around to see a cherry blonde following her. The woman was on the large side, like Angel and herself. It amazed her how many of the sweet-butts were always so slim. They did nothing but fuck the club members.

She stared at the other woman's bright smile.

"I thought you didn't hear me," the woman said.

Tate recognized her as one of the dental nurses. She was one that the other nurses mocked and called fatty.

"What do you want?" Tate asked.

"Erm, I noticed we lived in the same building, and I was wondering if you wanted some company on the way home?" The cherry blonde smiled, and her face was red, from embarrassment or from the running, Tate did not know.

"Do you know who I am?"

"Yeah, you're Tate Johnson."

"I'm not part of The Skulls. If you're hoping for a way in then go and find someone else. You can fuck your way into the club."

Cherry held her hands up. "No, I don't care about the club. I noticed you're not friends with anyone, and I wanted to offer *you* friendship."

Staring at her, Tate frowned. "What's your name?"

"Kelsey Ryan."

"Hi, Kelsey, come on then. Let's go home."

The other woman chuckled and started walking beside her. Tate was not used to women befriending her. Most of the women she'd come to know were always trying to work their way into the club and near the men. Thinking about it, so were the guys, but for another reason. They wanted to be members.

"Why don't you want to be part of The Skulls?" Tate asked, firing the question at the other woman.

"Seriously?" Kelsey asked.

"Every other woman would be trying to find a way to get close to the club. Why are you not asking questions?"

Kelsey tucked some of her cherry blonde hair behind her ear. "Erm, I'm not interested in the lifestyle or anything. I know what they do and everything. Besides, I'm not exactly biker woman material."

"The guys will fuck any willing female," Tate said, hating how mean she was being. After years of being used by people she thought were friends when they'd only ever wanted to know her to get to the club, she'd learned to become hard when making friends. There were only two people she'd never been hard on, Eva and Angel. The two women were completely different, and Tate treated them like that.

"I don't want to be part of any lifestyle. You're being unfair, and all I want to be is your friend." Kelsey looked behind her. "Look, I don't make a lot of friends, and I know they're not interested in being your friend. I know this must be hard and I accept that, but insulting me is not fair."

Feeling bad at the look of hurt coming from Kelsey, Tate smiled. "Okay, fine, we'll be friends." Hating the way she'd been, she turned to the woman and held her hand out in front of her. "Look, I'm really sorry. I've had a rough couple of weeks. Erm, I'm not used to people wanting to make friends with me." Murphy appearing on the scene was driving her crazy. She'd promised herself she wouldn't let herself feel anything.

Hiding behind her bitchy exterior was not helping. When she was alone, she allowed herself to hurt. In her apartment, away from Eva and everyone else, no one saw her pain. Murphy had hurt her in ways she couldn't describe, and even after all this time, she'd not been able to forget. Now with Murphy back, she couldn't handle seeing him every day. She was always reminded of their past together.

She stepped closer to Kelsey and started walking. With her away from the club, she really could use a friend. The sound of a motorbike roaring in the distance made Tate panic. She picked up her speed with her new friend trying to get to her apartment building. The only person who came to visit her was Murphy. It was like he was taunting her at every turn.

It was too late as the bike pulled in front of them on the path where they were walking. Without thinking Tate reached out and took Kelsey's hand, looking for support in whatever form she could find it. There was no running from Murphy with him stood right in front of her.

Recognizing the cut of the leather jacket, Tate waited for him to turn his focus on her.

The bike was turned off, and he climbed off. She watched him remove his helmet and turn those dark intense eyes toward her. Swallowing past the lump in her throat, she stared at Murphy, waiting. She tightened her hold on Kelsey.

"What the fuck are you doing?" he asked, looking at her and then at Kelsey.

"I'm walking home, which you're interrupting." Looking up at the sky, which had darkened in the last few minutes, Tate let out a curse. "If you don't get out of my way, I'm going to be cold, cranky, and you're going to be the cause." Inwardly she cringed at her actions. There were times she really hated being a bitch whereas other times she found it easier.

"I'll take my chances." His gaze turned to Kelsey. "Who's the cherry?" he asked.

Fisting her free hand, Tate glared at him. "My new girlfriend. I've decided men don't have what it takes."

"I've always loved a threesome."

His words hurt more than she wanted them to. Stepping closer, Tate raised her palm and slapped him around the face. Murphy didn't show any signs of caring. There was not so much as a flicker of emotion to cross his face. He stood there and did nothing.

"I think you've had enough fun. Stay away from me."

She led Kelsey around the bike and toward her home. In that moment she was bombarded by many more happy memories of them together, which only made her hurt more.

"Are you okay?" Kelsey whispered to her.

"No, I'm not okay."

"Your father misses you," Murphy said, shouting the words out to her.

"He's got the club. Tiny doesn't need me at all." Her words were mean, but she didn't care. Tate just wanted to get as far away from him as possible. She kept walking, and fortunately, Murphy didn't follow her. The sound of the bike starting up made her jump. Still, she kept walking with Kelsey beside her.

They made it to their apartment building, which was a few streets from the dental practice. Tate liked being able to walk to work and not having to rely on the club or a prospect. She was tired of always relying on someone else.

Kelsey opened the door for her.

"Thank you," Tate said. Her hands were shaking, but she kept moving forward, realizing the other woman hadn't followed her. Stopping she turned to Kelsey. "Are you coming up?"

"Erm, I'm on the ground floor. I don't like heights at all."

"Oh, well, you can come up for some coffee and food if you'd like?" Tate asked, suddenly not wanting to be alone.

"Okay. Only if you're sure?"

"I'm sure. Can you be on the fourth floor without fear?"

The other woman nodded. "Yes, I can handle the floor as long as I don't live there full time."

Smiling, Tate started up the stairs heading for her room. She needed the company. Murphy wouldn't try to see her with someone there. The club came first, and Kelsey was a civilian. She hated using the other woman like this, but it was the only way.

She's not the only person you've used.

Tate cut the thought off.

Once inside, Tate flicked the switch, illuminating the whole apartment. "It's not much, but it's home."

"I know. I'd rather live on my own than with my parents. They like things their own way, and I needed to spread my wings and live."

Agreeing, Tate moved toward her small kitchen. The space was always open, but she wasn't going to complain. The apartment had everything she needed. There was a bedroom, sitting room, kitchen, bathroom, and plenty of hot water for a bath. The building was also sanitary, which was a huge bonus. She hated bugs of all kinds and couldn't stand to think of bugs in her apartment.

"You can take your jacket off."

Kelsey removed her jacket, sitting in the seat that Tate pointed at.

"Your machine is buzzing," Kelsey said.

Glancing over to her answering machine she saw over fifteen messages blinking at her. The kettle was on, boiling. Pressing play, she began to listen, not caring that Kelsey was witnessing it. There was a lot she didn't care about.

"Tate, I swear if you don't get your fucking ass home, then you're in deep fucking trouble. I didn't raise you to be reckless. Stop behaving like a spoiled brat."

Tate rolled her eyes at her father's words. Tiny was not right about everything. If anything, he'd taught her to never take shit. He was a mass of contradictions, and she wasn't going to apologize for being number one.

"Tate, honey, your father is beside himself with worry. Please, talk to him and let him see you're fine."

Eva sounded far more understanding. The next two messages were from her father, and the couple after that were from Lash and Nash.

In the end, Tate deleted all the messages without listening to every single one.

"Your family care," Kelsey said.

"No, they don't. Well, they care. What they don't like is me putting myself first, not the club." Shaking her head at their insistence, Tate made her way back to the kitchen to finish their coffees. "So, Kelsey, tell me about yourself."

For the next hour Tate prepared food while listening to her new friend talk about herself. Kelsey liked to read, cook, and work. Tate liked her instantly as not once did she mention fucking or joining motorbike clubs in her spare time.

After they finished eating, both women cleaned away their dishes, and then Kelsey excused herself, offering to walk to work with her the next day. Tate accepted the company and sat back on her sofa staring at the clock. She was waiting for the knock or the unmistakable sound of her window opening or something. Murphy was a creature of habit, and she'd bet money he'd come out of her bedroom where her window was partially open for a little fresh air. Sipping her coffee, three minutes later her bedroom door opened.

"You've got to start leaving the window closed," he said, coming to stand in front of her. She stared down at his wet shoes making a mess on her carpet.

"Get your shoes off."

"No."

Shrugging, Tate didn't raise her voice. She sipped at her drink, waiting for him to speak now that he'd invaded her space.

"Cherry your new little friend, or have you switched sides?" Murphy asked. "Last time I knew you, you loved cock."

Tate truly believed she was a woman of the world. Growing up in a world of rough bikers who spoke without a filter she'd heard a lot of crap. Murphy's words didn't fail to make her cheeks heat.

"You're disgusting." Glancing up the length of his body, Tate ignored the jolt charging through her system. He really was a handsome man. No wonder women fell all over themselves for a chance to be with him. Murphy was a tall man, over six feet with muscles to go with his frame that people refused to argue with. She'd seen him hurt men twice the size of him without blinking. Remembering how he used to protect her during high school brought back too many memories. They were good memories, which made what he had done to her that much worse.

His hair was tied at the back. She knew it was only a matter of time before he cut it off. Murphy hated long hair. His face was clear of any facial hair. Murphy was perfect in size, looks, and attitude. She felt an awakening arousal deep in her core.

For a long time she'd pushed aside her sexual need, instead sticking to her anger. Around Murphy she couldn't control her reactions, and that hurt her more than anything.

Chapter Two

At twenty-eight years old, Murphy knew when a woman was fighting her arousal. Folding arms over breasts, rubbing together thighs, or lack of eye contact were all part of the fight, and his woman was displaying them all. Tate was aroused by him, and she was fighting it. He couldn't push too much. Their relationship hadn't been the same since he'd come back. His time at The Lions had changed a lot of things, including their relationship.

"I'm all for you wanting pussy, baby. It'll be fucking hot," Murphy said, unable to resist pushing her a little.

She glared up at him. His dark, hard temptress was close to the surface. Murphy knew Tate better than anyone else knew her. He knew which buttons to push and how to make her fight.

Within seconds she slammed the cup she was holding down on the coffee table. "You're fucking disgusting. Kelsey is my friend. She's probably the only woman in Fort Wills who doesn't want anything to do with the fucking club or with you."

Tate got to her feet, separating the short distance between them. Watching her, Murphy felt his cock respond in kind. She really was a fucking beauty when she was angry. He'd known her before the shit hit the fan, and part of him liked this woman just a little bit more. There was a fire within Tate that called to him. He wanted to go up in flames with her. He'd missed this, and he'd missed her. Tate was the only person who kept him going during the darkest moments at the other club. The Skulls were rough, but The Lions were deadly to all. Murphy did not regret his actions. Infiltrating their group he'd brought an end to their awful ways. The drink, the drugs, and the women were all too much.

"What are you doing here?" she asked, sitting back down.

"You've left your father's house and won't talk to him." He sat on the coffee table waiting for her response.

"The club? I shouldn't be surprised. All you think about is the club," Tate said.

Anyone else wouldn't detect the hurt in her voice. Murphy was the one who knew her. He'd been the prospect assigned to her protection.

"The club comes first, you know that."

He didn't see the coffee until it was too late. Tate poured the semi-hot coffee over his crotch. Gasping, he stood worried about his crown jewels.

"What the fuck, Tate?" Picking up the nearest cloth he tried to clean away the wetness from his dick. She could have seriously burnt him.

She stormed off, and he saw her getting a jacket on. "Come on then. Let's go and see dearest daddy, shall we?" Tate asked.

Tate was out the door. Cursing, Murphy ran after her, trying his best to keep up as she charged downstairs and out of the building. She was stood next to his bike with her arms folded.

"You're not in the right mind to be making this decision," he said.

"Fuck you. You've not been a Skull for a long time. You don't know me. You'll never know me."

Seeing no point in arguing, he straddled his bike and waited for her to do the same. Handing her his helmet, Murphy waited for her to wear it. It was his helmet, but he'd ride without it for her safety.

Gunning the engine, once her arms were wrapped around his waist, Murphy worked his way back to the club. The rain was light, and he got to the club without a problem. By the time he parked the bike, Tate was off and inside the club. He heard the shouting within minutes.

"You're my daughter. Don't you fucking talk to me like that," Tiny said.

"You were just fucking a woman my age. I don't give a fuck if I'm your daughter or not!"

Heading inside, he saw Tiny stood next to his office with his jeans open and the door shut.

Hardy and Rose were sat in the far corner watching, along with Angel and Lash. The others were gathered around the room watching what was happening. Murphy noticed Killer, Whizz, and Time watching as well.

"What happens at the club is none of your business."

"Then deal with me not being part of the club. I can't believe you. You've got a fucking minion looking out for me."

She pointed toward him. Murphy was insulted by her new title for him. Minion? He was no fucking minion.

"Tate, you're behaving like a spoilt little bitch."

"I don't give a fuck. I moved out. I don't need you anymore, and you can't handle that. I've got a job, and you're without a daughter."

"Eva is at home for you. What about her feelings?" Tiny asked.

"She's there because you're too much of a fucking pussy to do something about it. You should let her go find another job, but no, you've got her waiting at home for you while you're fucking everything in sight." There was no stopping Tate in her flow. He saw Tiny was tense as she hit home with what she was saying. "Eva deserves a man who'll be there for her and won't fuck everything with a hole. She deserves the kind of man Mom had. The man you no longer are."

Deadly silence settled over the club. Tiny's emotions shut down.

"What the fuck did you say?" Tiny asked.

Murphy had never seen his president hit a woman, but from the look in his eyes that could all change.

"Fuck you. Fuck the club. And if you were a decent man you'd let Eva go." Tate turned on her heel looking at all the club. "What the fuck are you looking at?"

"I'll cut you off, Tate."

"Do it. The further I'm away from this club and you the better I'll be." She turned at the last minute. "Oh, Tiny, I'll be letting Eva know the truth. This is the last woman's life you ruin."

She slammed the door closed. It was the first time she'd not called Tiny, Dad. Tiny was clearly in shock. In the next instant, Tiny slammed his fist against the wall. "Get her home safely," Tiny said, through gritted teeth.

Murphy watched as he pointed at Killer and ordered him to sort the woman out in his office.

"Get rid of the bitch. I don't care what you do, just get her out."

He headed outside to see Angel talking with Tate. Lash was stood smoking a cigarette watching the interplay.

"Tate won't let me near her. She doesn't want anything to do with me. Angel's the only person she'll talk to."

"She's being stubborn. Give it time and her mood will ease and she'll come back," Murphy said. He recognized her mood and had dealt with it before.

"I don't know. Something is different. She's not a teenage girl anymore wanting a pissing doll. This is serious. Tate's serious, and she's cutting everyone off." Lash turned to him. "The shit that went down with The Lions, it was bad?"

"Yeah, it was bad. I hate the fact I hurt her, but we needed to take them out. The Lions are bad news, and the sooner we cull the stragglers, the better."

"You're not going to talk about it?" Lash asked.

"No, never."

"Well, if it's not Lash and my other brother from another mother," Nash said, stumbling closer to them. Kate, a sweet-butt, was on his arm. One of her hands was inside Nash's jeans. "Tate, honey, you've got bitch written all over you."

Tate stuck her fingers in the air, swearing at Nash without saying a word.

"The two chubby women are together again," Kate said. Her eyes were glazed over. Murphy put it down to alcohol.

Nash pushed her away, making her trip. "Don't shit-talk them, bitch. You're a fucking whore after a good time, and don't forget your place."

"Nash?" Lash said, putting an arm out to his brother.

"No, she doesn't get to talk shit." Nash pushed his brother away.

Seeing the drama about to unfold, Murphy moved away. Nash had his own issues with Kate.

"Please, don't leave," Angel said.

"This is your world, Angel. I'm not part of it anymore. Come by my apartment this weekend, and we'll talk then." Tate hugged the other woman before pulling away. "Take me home."

He didn't say anything and climbed on the bike, waiting for her to get on behind him. The drive was short. He left his bike, following her upstairs. She didn't acknowledge him and went straight for the bedroom. Closing the door behind him, he watched as she opened a wardrobe and started going through the contents.

"Tate, you can't ignore me," Murphy said, trying to draw her out.

In answer, she grunted something. Rubbing a hand down his face, Murphy stepped into the room. Without thinking he opened a drawer, wanting to know something new about this woman. When he'd left Tate she'd been happy, all too ready to tell him her secrets. This Tate wouldn't give him a damn thing.

What he found made him pause. Lying in the bed of her underwear was a dildo. It was plain rubber or whatever dildos were made of. He saw the lube to go with the dildo. Moving the underwear around he saw another smaller dildo.

"You can stop snooping," she said.

Turning toward her, he saw two boxes in her arms.

"What the hell is this?"

He held the sex toys wondering what her response would be.

"That is Bob. He helped to be my first time. Virginity is overrated, and that's what I use for my ass."

Okay, she'd shocked him more than he expected.

"You think I was going to sit around waiting for you?" Tate snorted, putting the boxes back on the bed. She took her toys from his hands. "No man would have ever been good enough for Tiny. I used what was at my disposal."

"By fucking a fake cock?"

"You were fucking Lion whores." Her voice grew louder. "You've got no right to yell at me."

Dropping the toys into the drawer, he banded an arm around her waist, pulling her close. “No? You’re mine, Tate. You promised yourself to me.”

Tears filled her eyes, and she went lax in his arms. “You promised me a lot of things, Murphy. Remember those promises?” she asked.

He tensed.

“Do you remember your promise to put me first? To tell me when you were having to do business?”

There was nothing for him to say to stop her.

She pushed him away, and Murphy let her. “You broke all your promises, and in doing so, you lost me.”

“You’re mine.”

“No, I’m not.”

Tate shoved him out of her apartment. Murphy let her. Right now she wasn’t ready for him to fight. It took every ounce of willpower to leave her alone.

****

With very little sleep, Tate met Kelsey downstairs waiting for her. The other woman was dressed in her dental nursing uniform while Tate wore her receptionist clothes.

“You look like you had a rough night,” Kelsey said.

Sipping her coffee from the travel cup, Tate agreed. “It was a rough night. A shit night.”

“Do you want to talk about it?”

“No. Actually, give me your view on this.” They walked side by side. Tate loved the feel of the fresh air on her face. “You fall in love with a guy who’s always around. Yeah, he’s ordered to be around you and protect you, but you’re around each other all the time. You’re together so much you have feelings for each other. Then, when you think you’re ready to start a life together, he disappears, and you see him with another woman every day."

"Is he having sex with these women?"

"Yeah, he's having sex."

"I'd learn to move on and not have anything to do with a man who clearly thinks so little of me," Kelsey said.

"Exactly what I was thinking. I hope his dick will drop off."

Kelsey chuckled. "I bet."

They made it to the practice and promised to meet for lunch. Tate spent most of the morning ignoring everyone. A couple of the women tried to draw her into a conversation, which she ignored. She saw the questions in their eyes. Testing the waters she talked to a couple of women and saw through their act. They wanted to get to The Skulls, not be her friend.

At lunchtime Kelsey had to work through with a dentist on some kind of root canal. Going into town Tate picked up a sandwich and took a seat on the nearest bench.

Eating her sandwich, she watched the world go by. An hour for lunch was long enough. When she saw Lash and Angel approaching on his bike, she tried to finish eating her sandwich.

Too late, Angel bounced over to her. "Hey, Tate, what are you doing?"

The other woman accepted the club life too easily. Angel was nice, but Tate needed to move on. "I'm on break. I've got to get back to work."

She stood, brushing the crumbs down her body.

"You're seriously going to cut everyone off?" Lash asked.

Tate hesitated. The Skulls were her family. "I've got to get back to work."

Leaving them on the street, Tate headed back to the surgery where she was working until late in the afternoon. She saw Kelsey nibbling on a sandwich when she returned. The waiting room was full.

"Hey, how are you doing?" Kelsey asked.

She needed to get used to having a friend. Angel and Eva were both her friends, but they came with the club. Why was it so hard for everyone to understand that she wanted some time away from it?

"I'm doing good. You?"

"It has been a busy morning." Kelsey let out a sigh. Looking over Kelsey's shoulder she saw the other nurses and receptionists chuckling.

"What's going on?" Tate asked.

"Your father is in with Dr. Bixton, and he's causing up a storm."

"What?" Tate looked toward the young doctor's door. There was no sign of her father, and no sound coming from the room.

"It's nothing. I don't think he's here for you," Kelsey said.

Tate removed her jacket taking a seat behind the desk. Great, this was not what she wanted to deal with right now.

Get out of Fort Wills.

The idea struck her, but she couldn't do it.

"Hey, do you want to get out of here for a couple of days this weekend?" Tate asked. Kelsey was still waiting.

"What? Get out of Fort Wills?"

"Yeah, let's go to Vegas and go wild?" Tate liked the idea the more she thought about it.

"Okay, that sounds a little reckless to me."

"How old are you, Kelsey? I'm twenty-four, and I'm feeling a little too old for my age. I don't want to feel old. We've got the rest of our lives to settle down. Let's go and be wild. You've got the weekend off, right?"

"Yes."

"Then come out with me?" Tate begged her new friend already knowing she was going to invite Eva as well.

"What the hell, why not? Let's go to Vegas."

Tate let out a whoop as Tiny left the dentist's office. He looked angry and stopped when he saw her.

"I want a word, Tate," he said.

"I'm working. I can't have a word." Tate ruffled some paper trying to make out how busy she was.

"Hi, Tiny," one of the nurses said, thrusting out her chest.

Rolling her eyes, she stared at her father.

"You can go with him, Tate," Dr. Brixton said, leaving his office.

Letting out a sigh, she followed her father out of the building.

"You've got the nurses chasing after you as well, great," she said.

He grabbed her arm, tugging her toward the alleyway so they could have some privacy. Walking out she noticed several of the other club members waiting for her father.

"Why are you being so difficult?" he asked. It was only them, and there was no angry father staring back at her. She hated this part of him. The part she got to see when they were alone and the guy he showed Eva when he felt like it.

"I'm taking control of my life, Dad. Why can't you see that?"

"The club is your life." He pulled out the necklace she'd sent back to him last night with Murphy. The necklace held her name in the center. At the time she'd loved it. Now it just hurt her too much to wear it. It was the necklace he'd given her when she turned sixteen and had once meant so much to her. "Why are you giving me this?"

She refused to take it. "Do you remember what you told me when you gave me that necklace?"

Tiny frowned at her, letting her know he'd forgotten.

"Forget it. I love you, Dad but I can't handle this."

"Is this about Murphy?" Tiny asked.

Closing her eyes, Tate counted to ten. "It's about so much more than Murphy."

"I know you've got feelings for him."

Shaking her head, Tate went to leave. He grabbed her arm stopping her retreat. "Don't walk away from me, Tate."

"Did Mom really accept coming second best to your club?"

Tiny reeled back as if her words had smacked him. "What's your fucking point?"

"I'm just wondering if you realized how much pain you were causing her." Tate put her hands on hips and glared at him.

"I've given you some room and allowed you to get away with shit because you're my daughter. My patience is running out."

"Fine. Let it run out. You know, one of my only memories of Mom is her on the couch, crying. She was staring at the phone, holding one of your cuts. In fact, I found her a lot of the time lying out on the sofa holding one of your cuts. The club comes first. I don't think Mom accepted it. She didn't have a choice, but I do."

Storming back inside Tate realized she'd not resolved anything with her father. She thought her problems came from her hurt with Murphy. Blanking out everyone else she focused on her own feelings while thinking about her father. Tiny had been a great father to her, but the club really did come first. Pushing the hair out of her eyes, she tried to put some reasoning to her problems. She loved her father. He was the one person she could count on.

After work she walked home with Kelsey, making sure she got home safely and then made her way toward her father's house. The house was large, and she'd gotten over the fear of The Lions bursting through the door. Seeing all of the men killed helped to ease her thoughts. For a few weeks she'd been shaken whenever the door rang, but nothing else came from it.

Eva answered the door at her knock.

"Honey, I've been waiting for you to get back in touch." Eva invited her into the house with open arms.

"I didn't know if he'd ban me from the house," Tate said, smiling.

"I wouldn't care if he did. Tiny's insensitive at times, and he does my head in. I wonder what he'll think if I just shoot him," Eva said.

"Does he know you own a gun?"

"Nope, I doubt he'll treat me any better. So, what brings you here tonight?" Eva pushed her into the nearest chair. The woman was only a couple of years older than she was, but Tate had bonded to the woman the moment she walked through the door.

Given half the chance, Eva would be an amazing mother.

"I'm going to Vegas with a girl from work. I was hoping you'd come with us."

Eva stared at her. "Tiny doesn't know about this?"

"No."

"You're not going to invite Angel?" Eva asked.

"No, I don't want anyone to know."

A glass of juice was placed in front of her as Eva stared at her. The other woman was beautiful. Her hair was dark and glossy, and she had the bluest eyes Tate had ever seen. "You want me to lie to your father?"

"Yesterday I caught him fucking one of the sweet-butts in his office."

Her words hurt. Eva flinched away, turning toward the stove. There was nothing for the other woman to do. "What he does is his own business."

"You're in love with him, and you're not going to fight for your man."

"Tiny is not mine. I'm your nanny. Nothing else."

"Good, then come to Vegas with me. Get away from all this shit."

"Language, Tate."

"Come with me."

"Are you doing this to upset your father? To get back at him over the Murphy thing?"

"No, I'm doing this to get away from everything else."

Eva stared at her, clearly considering the options. "Fine, I'll come with you."

Great, a weekend away with no club members and only the girls. Tate couldn't wait for the fun to begin.

MURPHY

Chapter Three

Murphy glanced around the abandoned warehouse as the rest of The Lions considered what they were going to do. There were so many pictures of The Skulls that he'd lost count. Pictures of Tiny, Lash, and Nash along with the rest of the club. There were also several picture of Tate. The ones of his girl caught his eye. They must have been taken recently because she looked ill. He knew how she felt as he felt the same whenever he was away from her.

Suddenly the image changed, and he was standing in Tiny's house staring at a scared Tate. A shot rang out, and then only he and Tate stood. One single shot to the stomach, and she looked at him with tears running down her eyes.

"You broke your promise, Dillon."

Gasping for breath Murphy shot awake in bed. The dreams were always the same and always a pain in the ass. Tate was always hurt, and he was always the failure. He hated the dreams more than anything else. Tate hadn't been shot. Eva, Angel, Steven, and Blaine had been shot. She was okay, and nothing was going to happen to her.

Flinging the blanket off his body, he padded into his bathroom to freshen up. After doing his business down the toilet, he washed his hands and began to brush his teeth. He rubbed his abdomen where he'd gotten his recent tattoo. Glancing down, he saw it was healing nicely, and he wasn't too concerned. The fancy writing across his abdomen, above his cock, was Tate. He'd gotten her name inked the moment his shit with The Lions was over. Murphy couldn't risk inking his body when he was part of the other club. They'd ask too many questions.

When he finished his shower, he headed down to the kitchen where the scents of burning food met him. Lash wouldn't let Angel cook. With Eva not allowed to visit the club and Tate gone, the food was being ruined by the sweet-butts. He couldn't stomach the smell, let alone the taste and settled on cereal.

Rose and Hardy were at the table talking. Angel was eating cereal and sat on Lash's lap while Nash grumbled about something. Tiny sat at the head, eating toast and flicking through the day's paper. Murphy stayed silent as Killer joined him. Whizz and Time followed suit leaving the women to murder food.

"I don't like Fern," Killer said.

"She's a bitch and probably has some disease. If you're desperate I'd put a rubber on," Murphy said.

"I heard that."

Before he got involved with Tate, Murphy had been shacking up with Fern working off the desire to fuck his president's daughter. He was the only guy who had stood up for Tate when she was younger. If he'd not stuck up for Tate, she'd never have gone to prom or any of the birthday parties she wanted to go. It was a good job Tiny hadn't found out about any of the other parties she'd sneaked off to.

"How are you boys settling in?" Murphy asked. Out of all of The Lions these were the three men who'd stuck out. They were not like the other club men. He knew given half a chance, Killer, Whizz, and Time would be great to the club.

"We've got prospect work. Looking after women, getting the groceries, even passing fucking messages onto law enforcement," Time said. The words were muffled as he was eating cereal while he did it.

The smell was getting worse from the kitchen. Female screeching was also getting louder.

"That shit fucking stinks," Rose said, shouting to be heard.

"I did tell Lash I didn't need to be escorted to the salon," Angel said, cutting through the chaos to answer Time. The other man picked up at being spoken to. Murphy saw the interest in the man's eyes and kicked him under the table. He'd have to have a word with the newbies. No one, not even a club member, fucked with an old lady. Angel was engaged, and it would only be a matter of time before Lash owned every inch of her.

"I thought Tate went to the salon with you," Rose said.

"She used to. I found out from reception that she cancelled her appointments and membership. I've not got anyone to go with." Angel's voice was small.

Even with his time spent with The Lions, Murphy knew the two women had gotten close. Was that why she was latching onto that new girl, Cherry?

"Tate cancelled her membership at the salon?" Tiny asked.

Angel nodded.

"Fuck!" Tiny stormed away. He was doing that a lot just recently. Murphy didn't point it out to him. He liked living with his genitals.

"Did I say something wrong?" Angel asked.

"No, baby. He's having a hard time dealing with Tate. If she was a boy, Tiny would have kicked his ass by now. Tate's different, and Tiny won't hurt her."

It was the truth, but Murphy was starting to think Tate needed a good fucking spanking to put her firmly in her place.

"What's on the schedule for today?" Murphy asked.

"Not a lot. We're hunting for the missing Lions and then dealing with our next ride," Lash said.

Nash stood up from the table and walked away.

"What's wrong with him?"

"Girl problems I bet," Lash said, smirking.

"Kate's not been by for a couple of days. He's feeling lonely." Angel answered the question, getting up from Lash's lap to get rid of the bowls.

He had enough of the problems circling the room. Murphy left the club and walked toward his bike. Glancing behind him, he saw Time had followed him. "What are you doing?"

"Why did you give me that look inside?"

"Angel's taken. The Lions shared everything. Their women, their drugs, their booze, but we don't. We're a family. Brothers, and you don't go fucking another brother's woman."

"Man, I wasn't doing anything."

"You were looking at Angel like you wanted to eat her pussy. I'm telling you don't. Lash has a short fuse, and if he thinks you're wanting a piece of his woman, he'll fuck you over."

Straddling his bike, Murphy nodded at him. "Don't mess with another brother's woman. It's a rule. Follow it, know it, and embrace it."

He left the club and gunned down the street heading toward the dental practice where Tate worked. This was not the life she ever wanted. He didn't care what she was spouting out at everyone. Tate had always wanted to be an old lady and follow in his mother's footsteps. It's what she'd told him, and it had been one of his promises to her, to make her his old lady.

Before he did anything else, he needed to know there was something between him and Tate. Parking his bike outside the dentist, Murphy waited for Tate to appear. Checking his watch, he saw it was a little before twelve. With the nightmares he'd been sleeping when he dropped, which usually meant early in the morning or later in the day. Drinking didn't help settle the demons either. It was like he was being haunted by his past and present.

By the time twelve came, several women left the building. A couple of them gave him a once over and even dared to approach him.

"Hey, handsome, are you looking for someone?" she asked.

"Yeah, Tate Johnson, where is she?"

The woman laughed. "It's her day off. I heard her and the other fat one say they were going away for the weekend."

"What did you say?" Murphy asked. All of his protective instincts came roaring to life. He'd listened to the girls at school bully Tate because of her weight. How had the shit extended into the work place? Didn't they see how fucking sexy she was? Her tits were huge, big enough to fill his hands and spill over. Every part of Tate was soft. He wasn't afraid of hurting her when they were messing around with each other. Many a night he'd lain in bed thinking about her ripe, full rounded curves snuggled against him.

Prom night had ended with them alone. He'd comforted her the whole night as she talked the whole night. When she'd suggested that she was ready, he'd panicked. He'd been torn in two wanting to take her, but he'd listened to the good part of himself and not taken her to bed. Murphy had always felt protective of her..

The woman laughed, clearly not seeing the danger in front of her. She batted her eyelashes at him, licking her lips that had too much lipstick on. "Come on, I can handle you better than two chubby women."

Reaching up, he stroked her face. The action deceived his enemy, and he grabbed her chin with such force she was gasping. Pulling her close he whispered the words harshly in her ear. "Listen to me, you fucking slut. I wouldn't bang you if you were the last woman on earth. The sight of you sickens me. You know who I am, and you know what club I belong to. If I hear you causing shit for Tate or Cherry again then I'll hunt you down and hurt you. I'll make sure they could never identify your body."

Staring into her eyes he saw the fear. Many times during Tate's high school years he'd done and said something similar to a friend.

"Do I make myself clear?" he asked.

"Yes, perfectly clear."

"Good. We didn't have this conversation, and I think you better spread the word out about Tate. She may not wear the patch, but she's a fucking Skull. You cross her, hurt her, and I'll fucking kill you."

Letting her go, Murphy watched the woman fall to the floor gasping. Several people gaped at him. He ignored them. The Skulls owned this town. The club kept the town safe, and every single resident knew not to cross one of them. Maybe it was time they all had a message that The Skulls were not soft.

His cell phone rang. Staring at the woman, Murphy didn't take his eyes off her.

"What?" he asked, answering the call.

"You're needed back at the club," Nash said.

"Why? I'm on Tate duty."

"Tiny's losing it. Tate and Eva have boarded a plane to Vegas. He's fucking causing problems, and he's ready to kill someone."

Perfect. Tate knew when to cause problems. Pocketing his cell he gave one last warning look at the woman before he rode away back to the club.

****

Eva paid for the best hotel room they could get. Tate paid a third of it, and so did Kelsey. She liked the fact Eva and Kelsey was hitting it off. The two women were constantly chatting, and it gave Tate a break. She was able to sit back without having to think about what to say next. The plane ride went without a hitch.

Part of her couldn't believe they'd made it out of town without any of The Skulls stopping them. Tate knew it would only be a matter of time before they were hot on their heels.

"This place is amazing," Kelsey said, flopping down onto the large bed. Eva was putting away some of their clothes.

"I got a discount. Tiny knows the owner, and he was happy to let us stay and party in his casino."

Tate frowned, looking at her old nanny. "What guy? I don't remember him knowing someone in Vegas."

She saw the flush to Eva's cheeks. "Tiny brought me out here once before when you went away for college. This happened before you decided college wasn't for you."

"Who's the guy?" Tate asked.

"It's Alexander Allen."

Recognizing the name, Tate moved toward the window. "He's my mother's brother?" She'd not seen Uncle Alex in such a long time. Her last memory of him was of an argument he was having with Tiny.

"Yeah, he wants a chance to see you, Tate. I agreed that you'd want to meet him."

Smiling, Tate nodded. She'd meet with her uncle, and then she'd party until the sun came up. The sun was already down, so there was not much time left of Friday.

"Okay, ladies, let's get ready for some serious partying and gambling." Tate went to the wardrobe grabbing the red dress she'd worn to her first club party. It was the same party she'd danced on the tables at the club with Angel. Guilt hit her in the chest for not inviting Angel. The young blonde wouldn't hold a grudge, but she'd be hurt.

She made a note to deal with Angel when she returned home. Eva came out of the bathroom wearing a purple dress that complemented her fuller figure. Her brown hair was pulled up off her neck and fell around her head in waves. Kelsey wore a long denim skirt with a blue shirt. Her hair was left down. Tate didn't realize how long the other woman's hair was. The tips of the hair brushed Kelsey's butt.

"Are we ready to have some fun?" Tate asked.

Both women agreed. The atmosphere was rather stilted. Tate hoped after a few drinks they'd relax a little. Nothing could happen to them other than fun.

They headed toward the elevator and waited to be let on. The doors opened revealing a middle aged man with greying hair. He was the same age as her father, but where Tiny wore leathers or denim, this man wore a designer suit.

She recognized him instantly as her uncle. Alex stood looking at her. His gaze admired Eva's body before settling on her.

"Hello, Tate," he said, ignoring the other two women.

"Hello, Uncle." Getting onto the elevator Tate couldn't stop her body tensing.

"Eva, I've credited this card. Use it at all the tables and play sensibly. Don't interact with men surrounded with bodyguards. It's not a good weekend for you to be here." Alex presented Eva with an envelope.

"You really didn't need to do this, Alex," Eva said.

"Take it. I'm doing this for Tiny and for Patricia." Alex didn't look her way. "I'm going to take my niece for a drink. Will that be okay for you?"

"Yes. Tate, are you happy with that?"

"Sure. I'll meet you on the floor, okay?" she asked Kelsey.

"Yeah. Erm, this is going to be fun, right?" Kelsey lowered her voice and looked between Eva and Alex. "Right now it's not a lot of fun."

Laughing, Tate wrapped her arm around her new friend. "We'll have so much fun you'll be talking about it well into old age."

Kelsey smiled back at her. When the elevator hit the ground floor, Tate noticed the three men waiting. She promised to meet the other two when she was finished with Alex. The three men followed them to the bar.

"Are they with you?" she asked, stepping in beside him.

"I'm a powerful man."

"A powerful man shouldn't be worried with three bodyguards."

Alex led them to the end of the bar. She took the seat next to him as he signaled the female bartender. Resting her elbows on the counter she waited to be served. Alex ordered her vodka with orange while he took a brandy.

"I've got many enemies. I'm not a good man, Tate. I'm a powerful man that does bad things," Alex said.

Lifting the glass to her lips Tate stared at him over the rim. "Why are you telling me this?"

"You're family, and unlike Tiny, I think you have a right to know the truth."

Putting the glass down, Tate couldn't look away. Staring at him now, she saw the threat within his depths.

This man was not a good man like he said. She remembered him buying her balloons for her birthday and being there for barbeques, picnics, Christmases, and birthdays.

"Are you with some kind of mob?" she asked.

"No. I'm in business with your father. He helps transport product while I pocket a hefty profit, as does he. Your mother met him on one of our business meetings."

"You're in business with my father?"

"No, I lied again. Tiny and I agreed you'd never find out. We're more than in business together, we're business partners. Tiny owns half of this building, and I was once part of The Skulls."

Tate finally sipped at her drink. She'd always thought Tiny was just part of The Skulls, the club that helped look after Fort Wills. She wasn't stupid and knew the club wasn't entirely legal.

"Start from the beginning."

"Patricia and I originally came from Fort Wills. She was too young to remember Tiny, but our parents left the town. It was too rough, drugs, prostitutes, bad vibes, everything. I started this place up, and Tiny came to me with an idea. He still lived in the town and had grown up watching it get fucked over by chaos."

Tate listened, knowing Fort Wills hadn't always been the quiet, placid town it now was.

"He had an idea, an idea that put a club in charge of Fort Wills. There were some men who wanted the same."

"Mikey? He was one?" she asked.

"Yeah, he was a hard nut back in the day. He was amazing at bringing order to the town. We offered him the chance of being leader, the president, but he turned it down. Tiny was the leader. He was the right man for the job. I was the business side, the muscle whereas Tiny knew everything about the town. One visit here, he met Patricia. She was young, sweet, innocent, and they fell in love with each other. I didn't want her to be part of it. Tiny wouldn't hear any of it."

"I know this. They fell in love, and he moved her back to Fort Wills."

"The club always came first. My sister accepted that."

"Do you own like drugs and prostitutes and everything you fought against?" Tate asked.

"No, Tiny and I move the drugs away from the town. We don't accept that shit going down in Fort Wills. We have a lot of crap going down. You don't need to know everything, but we've both made a lot of enemies. He's got the club to protect him, and I've got my men. They're loyal."

"Why did you stop coming when Mom died?"

"We thought it was best you having a clean break. You weren't attached, and we had business that kept me out of town. Tiny didn't want you part of any of it." Alex sipped at his brandy, stopping.

"So that's the story?" Tate asked.

"Pretty much."

"It's fucking lame." Tate stood ready to leave. "The Skulls are a family. When Mom died you had a choice. I thought you blamed us. I thought you hated Dad so much that you couldn't bear to see us."

"Sit down, Tate."

"No, I'm done being ordered around by men who think they own me. I'm going to go and party. I don't want you to come near me."

"I was hoping we could build a friendship up," Alex said. "You're the only thing I've got left of Patricia."

"You should have thought about that before you put the club first."

She walked away. What was it with the men who put the club first? Alex could pretty up his explanation all he wanted. He still put the club first. He chose business before getting to know her. She'd grown up thinking her uncle didn't love her after her mother died.

Shaking her head, she found Eva at one of the machines with the pulley at the side. It looked boring.

"Are you all right?" Eva asked.

"No, I need alcohol, partying, and dancing, and I need it now."

"Alex loves you, Tate."

"No, he doesn't. Like Dad, Murphy, Lash, Nash, and all of the fucking Skulls, they're in love with the club. Maybe it'll do them more good to fuck each other instead of putting us through hell."

Kelsey giggled beside her. "Now that would be fun to watch."

"Does this place have a dance floor and bar away from the gambling?" Tate asked.

"Yeah."

"Lead the way, Eva. It's about fun. Fun and nothing to do with the club."

Chapter Four

Murphy walked off the plane four hours after Eva, Tate, and Cherry had gotten off. That was four hours of trouble his woman could already be in. A long, sleek black limousine was waiting for them. Killer followed close by Murphy as they climbed inside. Hearing about the women's expedition, Tiny had gathered six men and one woman to go to Vegas. He and Killer were there, along with Nash, Lash, Tiny, and Zero. Angel was travelling with Lash, even though Tiny had rejected the idea of another woman getting involved.

"I swear when I find her and get her alone she's going over my knee," Tiny said.

"Tate won't let you get that far," Lash said, smirking.

"I wasn't talking about Tate. Eva's going over my knee for a fucking spanking. The woman should have told me what was happening. Keeping shit from me is not acceptable."

Looking around the back of the limousine, Murphy saw all of the men were trying to contain their laughter. Eva and Tiny were destined to be together. Tiny was being a hard ass by keeping her at arms' length.

"Of all the fucking places to come, she had to choose Alex's casino." Tiny was muttering to himself.

"Who's Eva?" Killer asked.

"Tate's ex-nanny. Tiny has a thing for her, but he keeps her away from the club."

"He fucks everything that moves. The woman I took out of his office was tied down to the desk with her ass in the air. She was begging to be fucked," Killer said.

Murphy knew a lot about his president's sexual activities. Tiny was a dominant man with thoughts that the woman stayed at home while the men worked. It was an old-fashioned view, but it was what Tiny believed. Eva and Tiny were in for a rocky ride before they got together.

"You better have a handle on Tate," Tiny said, drawing him into conversation.

"I'll deal with Tate."

"I've called ahead. Alex is giving up rooms. It's a slow weekend in Vegas for him."

"I'm up for watching you spank Eva. It's going to be interesting. I wonder if she'll give into you willingly or if she'll put up a fight," Nash said, laughing.

Out of the two Myer brothers, Nash was the one who risked his life more. The guy must have a death wish by talking about watching Eva and Tiny together.

"With where your dick's been, you're not coming near Eva."

Nash stopped laughing. "My junk is clean. I don't touch anyone without a rubber. Speaking of where a dick's gone, what about yours, Tiny? You remembering to rubber up before the loving?"

Tiny launched himself across the limousine. One punch was thrown, and Nash was in the fight as well.

The other four men tried to pull the men apart in the small space. Angel was screaming, and Lash finally pulled Tiny away from his brother. "My brother deserves a beating, but I'm not having you put my woman in danger. Think, Tiny. He's fucking with you. It's Nash. Keep the anger locked up tight, or you're going to lose it too bad."

Slowly, minute by minute, Tiny calmed down to the point of relaxing. Nash's face was already bruising up.

"Sorry," Tiny said, sitting back down.

"Yeah, sorry. It was fucking wrong of me to talk like that," Nash said.

Everyone sat down, and silence fell over the group. The limousine couldn't move fast enough to get them out of trouble. They were confined to a moving vehicle with temperamental bikers, and that was a recipe for disaster.

"Four hours. Do you have any idea what damage Tate could do with four hours? Eva's not much better. She'll do anything for that girl, even lie to me about this fucking trip," Tiny said.

Murphy watched the city pass him by. Four hours with no one around Tate, he knew the damage was going to be dangerous. Visions of men fucking her, being inside her, and leaving her alone entered his thoughts. She was a fun woman and drew people to her when she wasn't such a bitch. Yes, some people gravitated towards her because of her position in the club, but there were still some who'd wanted to know his woman. He was all too aware of the draw of her. Over the years, looking after her, he'd tried to ignore her. She would talk to him for hours while she did homework. The hours she spent playing pranks on him had eventually made him fall into her web. Her taste in movies was also different. She was the only woman he knew who would watch a horror flick and then be crying at a romantic comedy straight after. He would wake up in the morning looking forward to spending the day with Tate. When she wasn't at school he found it fun to just hang out with her at the mall or watching movies. She was just fun, and he'd ruined that part of her. Being in The Lions didn't mean he was lost to what was happening. He saw the damage he'd done on a weekly basis. Tate was no longer the carefree woman she'd been, and he was the one who had to deal with that every day.

There was a harshness to her. He'd asked the prospects assigned to looking after her, and all of them spoke of her ignoring them, even yelling at them to get away from her. She didn't let anyone near her or to get close. From what he'd learned, Angel had been the only person she'd gotten close enough to.

Not close enough to invite to Vegas.

Glancing over at Angel he saw the sadness in the other woman. She hadn't complained during the drive.

When he got his hands on Tate he was going to show her the damage she was causing to others. She could take her anger out on him but no one else.

The limousine stopped outside a tall, wide building. The lights were bright, illuminating the sky and pavement. Climbing out of the back, Murphy stared up at the busy building.

"I thought you said this was quiet," Murphy said.

"The hotel's quiet. The main casino is as busy as it should be for a Friday night." Tiny answered, looking up at the casino. "It has been too long since I came here last. Brings up too many fucked up memories."

"Patricia," Lash said, mouthing the words to him.

They were gaining a lot of attention. Their cuts had a lot of reputation, even in Vegas. Entering the casino, security intercepted them. Murphy tensed expecting a fight.

"Mr. Allen is waiting for you at the bar," the tallest man said. "If you and your people will follow me?"

Murphy followed beside Killer toward the bar section. A man with greying hair sat at the bar looking at the screen of a laptop.

The security man cleared his throat.

"Leave," Mr. Allen said.

"Alex, it's good to see you," Tiny said, embracing the man in a male hug.

"Your daughter's a tough cookie, Tiny. What did you do to her?" Alex looked at all of them. "You certainly brought the cavalry."

"These are my men, and that's Lash's woman, Angel. She's a friend of Tate's. Where's my daughter? I thought we agreed you'd keep her close."

Alex sighed, turning the laptop to face them. "I tried to talk to her. She's not the most understanding of women, Tiny. There's your daughter. I've got men watching her, and I've been keeping an eye on her as well."

Looking at the screen, Murphy lost it. Tate was on the dance floor wearing a slut red dress, which showcased all of her curves. Her tits bounced as she danced to the beat of the music, and his anger spiked.

"Where the fuck is she?" Murphy asked. Tiny let out a growl and turned away.

"If I was you, I'd follow him," Alex said.

Killer followed him as he went after Tiny. The older man took the stairs leading down to the base of the club.

"Alex installed a nightclub. It's popular, but it's downstairs and the guards will only let certain people in," Tiny said.

"You mean women who are ready to fuck?" Murphy asked.

"Get Tate out of there. I'll handle Eva. You, Killer, get the other girl out of there." Tiny gave his orders as they got to the door. The guy on the door was talking into his ear piece. He held his hand up, listening.

Tiny was about to give orders when the guy opened the door. "You'll have no problems from us while you get your women out."

"I don't want to hurt anyone," Killer said. "Not a woman. Not again."

"She's Tate's friend. Just get her out. She looks submissive enough that she'll follow you."

Entering the darkened room, Murphy waited for his vision to adjust to the lack of light. Tiny left them heading toward Eva, who Murphy saw was stood at the bar. Looking onto the dance floor, Murphy spotted his own woman. His cock got hard at the sight of her lost to the music. Her friend was dancing with her.

He pointed out the friend to Killer. "Get her, get out. Go to Alex, and he'll give you the necessary keys to the rooms where we're staying."

Killer left his side, and Murphy concentrated on Tate. Her eyes were closed as a guy humped away behind her. Clothes were in the way of any real action. He blocked the guy out and simply admired his woman.

Her body was a thing of beauty. He loved watching her. Everything was natural. Her tits bounced, her hips swung from side to side. She was all woman, and he was about to get her for himself.

Moving around behind the guy, Murphy shoved him away, relishing the curse from the other man. He wanted the other man to get up and fight him. Instead, the guy took one look at him and left. *Fucking coward.*

Wrapping an arm around Tate's stomach, he tugged her close, rubbing his hard dick against her ass.

She gasped, leaning back against him.

"You should have known I'd come for you," he said, whispering the words to her ear.

Tate turned in his arms, facing him. Her face was flushed, and the slight scent of alcohol radiated out of her.

"I was expecting it. I thought I'd get a night to pick up a man and you'd find me getting fucked by someone else." She wrapped her arms around his neck. This response he hadn't been expecting.

Inserting a leg between her thighs, Murphy raised it up until her crotch rubbed against him. She cried out, rubbing herself all over his thigh.

"I'm so wet, Murphy," she said.

Tate moved closer, licking his neck and then nibbling on him. Fuck, he was ready to come in his pants, and all she was doing was touching him.

Reaching down, he grabbed her ass and brought her closer to him still.

"Do you want to fuck me, Dillon?"

It had been so long since he'd heard his name on her lips. There was a time when it was all she called him.

"You know I do."

She leaned in close, biting on his neck. "It's a shame you put the club first because you could have been fucking me for the past few years."

Tate stepped back, caught him off guard and kneed him in the balls. "That's for picking them over me," she said, turning on her heel and walking away.

****

Getting out of the nightclub was Tate's main concern. She moved around the people and headed for the door. Gripping the handle she turned in time to see Tiny grasping Eva around the waist and hauling her up in his arms. Glancing over her shoulder Tate saw Murphy getting to his feet while cupping his balls.

She needed to get out of here before she did something she'd regret. Opening the door, she nodded at the doorman then raced up the stairs. Her heels were hindering her escape. Stopping, she removed her heels and took off through the casino. No one stopped her as she ran toward the doors that held the stairs for the hotel room.

For several seconds with Murphy's arms wrapped around her she'd been tempted to give in to him. Then reality hit her hard. Murphy was not the man who promised to love her and to put her before everyone else. He was the guy who'd left her without any explanation and then fucked any woman he wanted. The only thing she was thankful for was that she didn't have to watch him fucking the women. She'd seen him around town plenty of times with several women.

Pushing the thoughts, the pain, and even the guilt of just hurting him, Tate ran upstairs toward her room.

"Tate!" Murphy was close as he shouted her name.

Running up the stairs, Tate tried to run faster. His movements were faster than hers, and she was losing her breath. She'd never run from an ex before.

Opening the other door to her floor, she ran to the steps, pulling out the key from her breast that Eva had given her. Her hands shook as she tried to push the key into the lock.

Murphy slammed behind her. He pulled her into his arms, covering her mouth with his hand as she made to scream.

"You're not escaping me tonight." He put her on her feet with his hand still over her mouth.

She clawed at his arms, trying to get free of his hold. Murphy held her firm, opening the door and locking it behind himself.

Finally, he let her go.

Tate tripped over her feet and fell on the floor in a heap.

Glaring at him over her shoulder, she got up, panting for breath. She was satisfied to see him panting as well.

"After all those women you're still unfit?" she asked.

"I see your dildo's not working for you either. Your dress can't hide your tits, baby. They're rock hard."

He took a step closer to her. Before she could react his hand went between her thighs, touching her heated flesh. Gasping, Tate couldn't fight him. She wasn't wearing any underwear, and the air between them changed. Staring into his eyes, Tate felt his touch go from hard to soft. His fingers didn't probe at her but stroked.

She saw his face change as well. There was no longer a fierce look on his face. His other hand cupped her face, caressing her cheek.

The fight left her. Tate didn't have the energy to be angry anymore. All she felt was the lust and the pain at his betrayal. Gasping for breath, she allowed herself this one night. What happened in Vegas, stayed in Vegas, and for once she could have this without any fear.

Catching his face between her hands, she tugged him down. Smashing her lips against his, Tate took the kiss she wanted from his lips.

"Tate, baby, please," he said, breaking the kiss. "Let me explain."

She shook her head. "No, no explaining. No nothing."

"I'm sorry."

Pressing her lips to his, Tate cut off his apology. She couldn't listen to it now. There was no way she could listen to anything he said. Pushing the jacket from his shoulders, Tate fisted her hands in his shirt. This was what she wanted tonight, nothing else.

One night. One night without fear. One night without arguments.

Tate wanted one night to forget the past between them. Closing her eyes, she slid her tongue into his mouth and transported herself in her mind back to their first kiss. She went back to her prom night where some people had laughed at Murphy being her date. The night had been lame, the dance awful with crap music and crap awards people gave each other to remember the glory days. The only upside of the whole experience had been Murphy. He was by her side with his arms wrapped around her, and she'd relished every single second of it.

He'd taken her outside to look up at the stars, and the music was still beating out to where they stood. After they admitted their feelings to each other, Murphy held her close and they'd danced. She'd been caught by his gaze, and then his head had lowered. Like in a dream, he'd kissed her deeply, making love to her mouth.

Opening her eyes, Tate pulled away from him. She wanted her prom night before he got the call that pulled him away from her. It hadn't been the call that put him in The Lions nest. No, it had been the call that started it. She knew it as she looked at him, older, harder, and sexier than he'd been eight years ago.

Had it really only been eight years since her prom?

Counting back, she knew it was. Eight years without ever feeling his naked body against her. It was pitiful. She may use sex toys, but she'd never taken another man. In her heart and mind she'd been Murphy's woman. When he'd left without a word, breaking her heart, she hadn't been able to let anyone else get close to her. Licking her lips, she stepped out of his arms. Eight years was a long time to wait for him, too fucking long.

Swallowing past her nerves, she reached behind her loosening the zipper holding her dress together. If she gave herself to him then maybe she could finally move on and not spend her life dwelling on what might have been.

"Tate, what are you doing?" he asked.

"What does it look like I'm doing?" She wiggled out of the dress until it fell at her feet. Stepping out of the dress, she kicked it aside. Removing her bra, she threw that on top of the dress, facing him completely naked. Next, she released her hair from the clip binding her hair. "I'm getting ready to be fucked."

He didn't move or say anything. Smiling, she stepped closer. His jacket was on the floor, revealing his tattooed arms. She'd sat with him through each tattoo. Running her hands up his arms, she caressed over each design. They were intricate, beautiful, and they brought back memories of watching his body be marked.

"Tate." He said her name as if he was going to tell her stop.

Gripping the top if his shirt, she tore it from his body, cutting through his warning. She wasn't going to stop. Tonight she was going to have her one night with him.

"Where's Kelsey and Eva?" she asked.

"Tiny and Killer are taking care of them."

"Will Killer hurt her?"

"No."

"Good," she said, grabbing his buckle. "We're doing this tonight. Tell me you don't want to, and I'll stop. We'll stop, and nothing else happens."

Opening the buckle she pushed his jeans down his thighs revealing his thick cock to her touch.

She touched him, wrapping her fingers around his length and started to work him over. "Tell me to stop, Murphy. Turn around, walk out the door, and it'll be over. No more fighting, no problems."

Pick the club and walk away from me.

Tate didn't say the other words, but she thought them. Staring into his dark gaze she waited for him to still her movements. Holding her breath, she stared at him waiting.

Time seemed to stand still while she waited for him to speak.

He reached up, cupping her cheek with one hand as the other covered hers over his cock. “Harder,” he said.

Tightening her grip around his shaft, she worked him over as he pushed the jeans from his body.

“No past between us tonight.”

“Fine.”

Glancing down his body, she gasped as she caught sight of the slightly red skin around his abdomen. Her name was printed into his skin, and from the looks of it, he’d done it recently.

Not tonight. Don’t question it tonight.

Sex.

She pushed her curiosity away and looked up at him. Her experience with men was a big fat zero. A dildo did as she asked without any argument. Murphy wasn’t cold rubber. He was all male.

“When did you get the ink here?” he asked, pointing to the ivy decorating her hip and up under her breast. She’d gotten the ink when he’d left and she realized he wasn’t going to come back. The ink had been a split second decision when she’d caught him at the mall slobbering over another woman.

Tonight, only think about tonight.

No past.

“I got it when I was ready.”

He wanted to push for more. Covering his lips with a finger, she shushed him. Stepping away from him, she moved back until she found the bed.

Sitting down, she slid onto the bed, opening her legs. “Come and get me, Murphy.”

“No, Dillon. In this room, right now, you call me Dillon, not Murphy.”

"Okay, come and get me, Dillon." She loved his real name. Licking her lips, she had an idea. Sucking two of her fingers into her mouth, she stared at him as she pressed them between her thighs, stroking her clit.

Moaning, she caressed down, stroking her wet fingers into her cunt.

"Dillon," she said, gasping his name. She was so turned on. There was no way she'd survive the night without him fucking her. She needed a man.

He fisted his shaft, stepping closer.

Crying out, she was shocked as he gripped her ankle tugging her to the edge of the bed.

"We're doing this my way. You're not in charge, Tate. You'll do as you're told." His fingers sank into her hair, cupping the back of her neck. "And you're going to suck my cock, getting it nice and ready to claim your fucking cunt."

His words were harsh, but she loved them. She loved everything about him, which is what made it so hard to settle with him. Being second best was not going to be part of her life.

"Open those sweet lips," Murphy said.

She did as he asked, knowing there was only going to be pleasure in her submission to him.

He pushed the tip of his cock against her lips, brushing the head over her lips. Pre-cum coated her lips, and she licked them, swallowing him down.

Her arousal grew with the rough way he was tugging on her hair.

"So fucking dirty and perfect. I dreamt about this moment."

His cock pushed in the first inch. "Wrap those fingers around my dick and feed it into your mouth."

They were really doing this. Tate covered his cock with her fingers, waiting for his next instruction.

"Take more of me in this mouth. One night, baby, that's what you've given me. Prepare to be awake all night. I'm not wasting any of it sleeping." He slammed his cock deep, hitting the back of her throat. Before she could panic, he withdrew.

She knew in her heart it was going to be the best night of her life.

Chapter Five

Murphy felt her mouth relax letting him fuck her in smooth, hard strokes. When he hit the back of her throat, he pulled away, giving her time to breathe. He didn't want her to fear him. Stroking her cheek, he watched his cock disappear into the warmth of her mouth.

Looking across the room he saw the mini fridge. Pulling out of her mouth, he went to the fridge. He opened it up, taking out several cubes of ice from the small freezer. Going back to Tate he found her fingering her clit. Shaking his head, he pulled her hand from between her thighs.

Her lips were soaked with her arousal. Bringing them to his lips, he sucked the cream from the digits. It was his first real taste of her cream.

"I'm going to feast on your pussy soon. You're not coming until I say so." Gripping her hair once again, he pressed the ice to her lips. "Open up and suck on it."

She took the ice cube sucking on it. When she finished, Tate opened her mouth. He saw the cube was gone, and he fed his cock into her mouth. She moaned around his length.

Closing his eyes, Murphy counted to ten to try to contain his orgasm. Their first time together wasn't going to be him climaxing like a randy teenage boy.

"Do you like sucking my cock?" he asked, opening his eyes and staring back down at her.

Tate nodded with her mouth on his cock. He gave her the other ice cubes and gasped between each one when her lips were around him. Her mouth was heaven.

"How many other men's cocks have you had in this mouth?" he asked.

She pulled away glaring up at him. "How many women have tasted you on their lips?"

Knowing his answer would piss her off, he kept it to himself. She took his cock back, and for several minutes he watched her working his length. Her saliva coated his shaft, and the suction was amazing.

He really wanted to know the answer, but he wasn't going to get it tonight.

Tugging on her hair, he pulled her away from his cock. "Get on the bed. Spread your thighs."

She climbed on the bed, and he admired the curves of her ass. He wanted to fuck her there as well.

Tying his hair with a band on his wrist, he climbed on the bed settling between her thighs.

"What are you doing?" she asked.

Smiling, Murphy got his answer. No man had touched or known this body. There was no way for a woman who knew the touch of a man between her thighs to be hesitant. Tate was hesitant, and he felt like one smug bastard. He knew there couldn't have been another man. She never gave herself easily. The way she'd sucked his cock had made him jealous. No other man was going to feel how amazing her lips were. The only cock she'd be sucking was his.

"I'm going to show this pussy some much needed attention." He squeezed her thighs, watching her stomach quiver as he blew on the tiny thatch of hair covering her pussy. "I see the salon visits have come to an end. You'll start them back up when we get home."

"Fuck you. This is all you're getting from me," Tate said.

He'd see about that. If she thought he was going to be satisfied with one night with her then she was plain fucking stupid.

Murphy silenced her when he splayed open the lips of her sex. Her clit was swollen, peeking up at him, begging to be sucked. Mouth watering at the sight before him, he inhaled her musky feminine scent. He'd not gone down on a woman for so long. Tate would be his first woman in a long time.

Running a single finger through her cream soaked slit, Murphy watched her cry out. She was going to be blown away by his tongue.

"Your dildo has nothing on me, baby. It can't give you the kinds of pleasure I can."

Tate glared at him. Her fiery gaze went straight to his cock.

"My dildo doesn't talk back."

Smiling, Murphy disappeared between her thighs, licking around her clit down to press inside her open pussy. She cried out. The sound filled every sense, and out of the corner of his eye he saw her hand fist the sheets beside her body. Her toes curled around, and her hips jerked, smashing her cunt onto his tongue.

"Fuck," she said, whimpering.

"Zero to the fake cock, and one to me."

"Shut the fuck up." She growled at him.

His response was to suck her clit into his mouth watching her collapse onto the bed. Biting on the hard nub, he sawed his teeth together. It wouldn't hurt but create enough sensation between pain and pleasure. She wouldn't know how to handle what he was doing to her body.

Slamming two fingers into her cunt, he coated them with her juice and brought them back to press against her anus.

She pulled away, shaking her head. "I don't think so," she said.

"Baby, you've been answering all my questions with your responses. Now come here and let me lick your juicy cunt."

"You're not touching my ass."

"Tate, soon I'll be fucking your ass, and you'll be begging for me to go deeper, harder than ever before." Pushing her down to the bed, Murphy dived between her thighs, slurping everything she had to offer him. He didn't touch her ass straight away. Murphy licked, sucked, and bit down on her pussy sucking her wet lips and clit into his mouth. She thrashed on the bed, and he had no choice but to hold her steady with hands on her hips to finish sucking her flesh.

Her body was so sensitive to his touch.

He heard her curse, crying out for him to give her an orgasm.

"Does my baby need me to stop?" Murphy asked, leaning away.

She was soaking wet, and the sight filled him with pride. After everything going on between them, he still owned Tate's body. He hoped to regain her heart and trust. They would take a hell of a lot longer.

"No, I need you to make me come. The night's not getting any younger," Tate said, screaming at him.

Rearing back on the bed, Murphy grabbed his cock and brought the tip to her entrance. Before he could stop himself, he slammed deep inside her tight heat. Tate cried out, gripping his arms as he groaned. She was tight, burning hot, and so fucking perfect. Her new name would be his sweet perfection. There was no way she should feel so amazing. Sex was sex, and within one thrust, he was addicted to the feel, smell, and taste of Tate.

They were both panting for breath. Staring down at his woman, Murphy felt a deep possessive feeling claw at him. Tate was his woman. Yes, he'd fucked up, but he wasn't going to give her chance to push him away.

"I see my cock shuts you the fuck up." Leaning down, he kissed her lips forcing her to taste her pussy on his lips.

Pushing his tongue into her mouth, Murphy tried with all of his might to stop her from thinking about anything but the way he made her feel.

He lifted one thigh over his waist and then the other. “Tell me, baby, who’s better? The fake cock or me?”

He eased out of her only to thrust back inside. She cried out, pressing up to meet him.

“I’m not telling you.”

Her cunt squeezed him tighter than her mouth ever could.

“I won’t let you come until you answer me,” he said, warning her. “I can fuck you all night long without coming at all.”

“You bastard.”

“I always get what I want, Tate.”

“Your cock is better, but I prefer my dildo. It doesn’t talk back.”

He left her snug pussy to attack her clit with his tongue. Murphy didn’t let up. He felt like he was competing with a piece of fucking rubber. It was stupid of him, but he wanted her to be addicted to him.

Flicking her clit, he was relentless in his assault. Her orgasm was what he wanted to feel. Licking and sucking her into his mouth, Murphy pressed two fingers into her pussy and felt how close she was to orgasm.

“Come for me, baby,” he said, muttering the words against her nub.

Tate screamed as her orgasm gripped her. He kept on her clit, not letting up until he was satisfied. Her cream soaked his fingers making them nice and wet. Sliding them to her ass, he pressed on her anus. She gasped and moaned still in the throes of climax.

The tip of one finger slid into her ass, opening her up for him.

A taster was all he was giving her.

Releasing her body, he crawled up the bed and plunged back into her tight warmth.

****

This was a mistake. Tate should make him stop before it got any worse. No words came. She didn't want him to stop, and yet she wanted him to at the same time. Her body pulsed all over from what he'd done with his lips, and now the hard, hot brand of his cock was deep inside her.

She was conflicted inside. Staring up at him, Tate swallowed down the lump in her throat. Fuck, she was still in love with him. Seeing him with all the layers taken away and the tattoo of her name made it hard for her to focus on hating him.

Don't think. One night, only one night, remember that.

Giving herself an inner pep talk wasn't helping at all. Closing her eyes, she lifted her hips feeding his cock deeper into her.

"Tate, baby, look at me. No more fighting me. I've got you, and I promise I'm not letting you go."

"I promise you'll always come first. The club means nothing to me unless I've got you. You're my first, Tate."

His past words penetrated her thoughts.

Covering his mouth with her fingers, Tate shook her head. "No, no promises to me. Not tonight."

It looked like he was going to say something else, and she shook her head. "No!"

Why couldn't he see how hurtful his words were? He spoke them easily, but she'd been living The Skulls life a lot longer than he had. She wasn't a member, yet she'd learned to always be second best.

This was her first ever sexual experience, and he was ruining it.

"Please, stop and make this worth it," she said. If her heart was going to be smashed to smithereens in the morning then she was going to spend the night enjoying it.

"You don't think this is worth it?"

"I'm getting bored."

She lifted her head and rested her hands underneath her head, smiling up at him. Testing him was always a pleasure.

"You can be a bitch when you want to be," he said. He eased out of her, grabbing some pillows for her to rest behind. "Let's see how you handle watching us together."

Staring down at her exposed flesh, Tate watched him slide his cock through her slit. His cock was slick, and the wet sounds filled the air between them. Her cheeks heated at the noise.

Was she a sick fuck for wanting a man who cheated on her with many women?

Push thoughts away. Focus on the now.

When she wasn't drawn into old memories the sex was amazing, but when they invaded her thoughts, it became hard to focus.

I'm still wet though.

"Watch my cock," he said.

Keeping her gaze between her thighs she saw something so erotic she almost came from the sight alone. Her body opened up, and the thick length of his shaft slowly disappeared. While she watched him sink into her body, she felt him penetrate her cunt. It was the strangest thing to witness but the most pleasurable experience to feel.

"That's right, baby. Who does this pussy belong to?" he asked.

Biting on her lip, Tate refused to say the words. Her body was her own. She couldn't give it to him.

He rolled them over. She was on top of his body, and he slapped her ass. "Tell me who you belong to."

"Myself," she said, clenching her inner muscles around his shaft. She'd learned to do that on the dildo, and there was no way she was giving him the satisfaction of teaching her. No other man had touched her body, but she refused to give him the satisfaction of showing her stuff.

His hands gripped her hips, and he thrust deeper hitting her cervix, making her gasp. Closing her eyes, Tate tried to even out her breathing. The pleasure was too much verging on the point of pain. She didn't know if she should make him stop or get him to ride her harder. All the feelings were conflicting inside her. Not one point helped her to focus

"You feel me deep, baby?"

Opening her eyes she stared into his dark gaze. His eyes were locked on hers.

"I get it. You won't say the words, but I know the truth." Murphy thrust his hips in a single jolt action. She caught hold of his abdomen to try to steady herself. "I love the way your tits bounce. So fucking beautiful."

Murphy moved his grip from her hips going up to cup her breasts. She watched his dark, tanned hands touching her pale flesh. Not a flash of sunshine had seen her skin.

"Your cunt is so wet for me. I can feel you drowning my cock."

He was getting way too vocal making it hard for her to keep him away.

Just sex. Just sex.

She could rant to herself all the time, Tate knew the truth. This between them was more than just sex.

Tate squealed as he pinched her nipples, hard.

"That's right, Tate, squeeze my cock. I'll make it hurt for you in such a good way." He did the same to the other nipple and then pinched them together. Tate could only hold on to him. Her nipples were so sensitive that she lost all focus of keeping him out and away from her.

"Fuck, I need to taste you again."

With strength she didn't even know he possessed, Murphy lifted her off his cock and brought her directly over his mouth. She gasped, reaching for the headboard as she straddled his head, and he set to work inflaming the fire inside her. His tongue probed her heat, pushing in deep before sliding up to circle her clit. Murphy bit down on her clit, and she tried to pull away. He kept a hold of her hips, and no matter how many times she tried to tug away, he stilled her with his arms alone.

It wasn't fair. She wanted to scream, curse, and not be affected by the pleasure he was creating with his mouth.

Suddenly, Tate gave up fighting him and the pleasure. Staring down at his dark penetrating gaze, she just stopped fighting him. There was no need to fight him. It was a waste of time and energy. She wanted this, and Tate would make sure it was the one and only time she let herself be with him like this.

Gripping the headboard with new determination she took control and started thrusting her hips, moving her pussy on his tongue.

He worked her clit, licking and sucking her nub into his mouth. Tate closed her eyes, groaned and let the orgasm ride through her body. She cried out, letting the screams fill the silence in the room. Her orgasm crashed through her, and she rode it loving every peak.

Finally, he eased her off him, and within seconds she was under him. His cock slammed deep inside her, cutting off any other thought but the feelings he was creating within her body.

His chin was coated with her arousal, and his gaze blazed with passion.

"I'm going to spend hours licking your cunt. I don't want you wearing any panties. I want easy access."

She didn't dispute his statement. There was no need to cause an argument with him fucking her. Murphy would fight her decision, and that was fine. She'd been vulnerable to him once before, and she wouldn't let that happen ever again.

If he thought this would bring the old, trusting Tate back then he was mistaken.

"Shut up, and fuck me."

One of his arms went behind her neck as the other gripped her thigh, opening her up. "Give me your lips."

Leaning up she took his lips tasting her cream. Plunging her tongue into his mouth, Tate kissed him with a passion that surprised her.

Murphy claimed her hard, each stroke going deeper than the other. His cock was long, thick, and embedded to the hilt inside her. He was that deep it was on the verge of pain. She took every inch of him, loving every second that the pain turned into the most desirable pleasure.

He didn't look away from her through the entire time he was inside her. Murphy's gaze was on her at all times. She felt possessed by him, owned by him, and there was nothing for her to do other than be claimed.

Ever since prom she'd spent many nights thinking about their first time together. This was by far better than anything she could have thought up. He truly was a magnificent man with his rock hard body and porn star cock.

"You're my world, Tate Johnson," Murphy said. He reared back, plunging into her, rubbing over her g-spot. She didn't anticipate another orgasm and cried out as he threw her into another orgasm. Tate heard him join her. She felt the pulse and the jet as he released inside her body.

His whole body tensed up, and his eyes closed. The growl that left his lips was the cutest, yet strangest, thing she'd ever heard. Throughout it all, her body tingled all over from the pleasure.

Breathing deeply, she stared up at him.

Slowly, he collapsed on top of her body, his head cushioned between her breasts. The weight of him was uncomfortable, but she wasn't going to force him to move.

Hesitantly, she reached up, stroking his damp long hair.

"You need a haircut," she said, stroking the wet strands.

"I've just fucked your brains out, and you're thinking about a haircut?" He glanced up at her, smiling.

"I guess you didn't do a good enough job."

He reared up in the bed. His cock was still deep inside her even though he was flaccid now and not hard. "Then I guess we have to rectify that. I can't have you thinking about haircuts."

Murphy wrapped her legs around his waist. She watched what he was doing. His fingers went to the lips of her sex, and he opened them.

"Look at that precious jewel," he said.

She held her breath as he pressed his thumb to her clit. Her pussy responded instantly. Tate tightened around his length.

He was already getting hard again.

"I'm young, baby, I've got a lot of years left inside me."

Words failed her. What was she supposed to say to him?

He played with her clit until he was hard enough to fuck. "I think it's time we made this a little interesting," he said.

Tate groaned as he left her. She saw him look around the room and then find what he wanted. He disappeared from the room.

"What are you doing?" she asked.

Chapter Six

Murphy had wasted so much time already, and he had a lot to make up for. Grabbing the can of cream and the chocolate sauce from the fridge, he went back to find Tate lying on the bed. Her hands were caressing over her body as she stared up at the ceiling. Putting the food down silently on the floor he went and grabbed the chair, positioning it in front of the mirror.

"What are you doing?" she asked.

Turning toward her, he saw her sat up in bed with her hands on her lap.

"Touch yourself." He folded his arms and stood at the bottom of the bed.

"Why should I do that?" She crawled toward him. Murphy didn't know how it was possible, but his cock got hard at the sight of her tits hanging down and her curves all on display for him.

"'Cause I told you to and afterwards I'll make it worth your while."

One of her eyebrows rose up at him.

"Okay, I'll hold you to that," she said.

"You won't need to."

She lay back on the bed with her pussy directly facing him. Her saw her soaked flesh with their combined releases covering her. His seed was leaking out of her cunt, and another wave of possession slammed into him. Tate was his, and he wanted to mark her with his cum. He didn't want her to move without some of his cum leaking out of her body. It was sick of him to think like that, but it was what he wanted.

No one else could ever love this woman the way he did. He'd risked his life to save her and done everything in his power to keep her safe. There was no way he was letting her go. He'd take every beating Tiny wanted to give him. The entire club could take turns fucking him over, and he'd accept it because at the end of it all, he'd have Tate. She'd be in his life, loving him, and that's all he ever wanted from the first moment he saw her.

"Touch your tits and twist your nipples to give you the bite of pain you need," he said.

Gripping his erect flesh, he watched her follow his orders touching her body.

She moaned, and her legs fell open wider. Her cunt was weeping with arousal.

Licking his lips, Murphy waited for her as she stroked down her body and finally landed between her spread thighs. Her fingers opened the lips of her pussy, and another finger slid inside her tight heat.

He watched her finger fuck herself, and he loved it.

His little ex-virgin was a passionate woman. Murphy saw it in her responses and the way she gave herself over to the pleasure.

"Oh, please, Dillon, fuck me again," she said, groaning as she did.

"Not yet." He took her hand away from her body. Lifting the chocolate sauce from the floor he dribbled some onto her body. He created a path from her navel all the way up to her breasts.

Dipping his head, he licked the sauce from her body.

"You're turning me into a candy stick," she said.

"No." He drizzled some chocolate sauce onto his cock. "This is a candy stick." He presented his covered shaft to her lips. "Lick it clean."

She opened her lips, accepting him as he sank into her mouth. Her tongue licked the sauce from his cock, and she moaned as she did.

He grabbed the cream and did the same with her breasts, coating them and sucking them off in between covering his shaft and feeding it to her.

Every now and again, he felt her stroking over the tattoo of her name. She didn't say a word about it.

When the taste of chocolate sauce and cream was too much for him, he took her hand and led her toward the chair in front of the mirror along the wardrobe.

He sat down and brought her down on his lap.

"What are you doing?" she asked. Her gaze didn't glance at their reflections. She looked at him over her shoulder.

"Look at yourself," he said.

He moved her thighs to the outside of his legs, and he opened her wide. Staring in the mirror, Murphy saw her red, swollen flesh clearly. She was amazing. He caressed two fingers through her silken slit, feeling her tense in his arms.

"I don't need to look in a mirror," she said.

"I don't care what you need or don't need. I'm telling you to look in the mirror, or I won't let you come again for a long time."

Murphy released her pussy, placing his hand on her thigh.

She glared at him. "You're not playing fair."

"I don't play fair. This is how I roll, baby. I get what I want by doing everything but playing fair."

Tate rolled her eyes. It was a battle of wills, and Murphy knew how to win. He stroked her thigh without going near where she wanted him to touch.

Soon her gaze wondered over to the mirror. He traced the tattoo going up and around her side and waist. It was a beautiful design, and he wished he'd been with her when she had it done.

He wondered if her father knew. Tiny would go ballistic if he knew. The guy was old fashioned like that.

"Why am I looking at us?" she asked.

"I want you to watch me play with you." He dipped down, sinking a finger inside her core.

"I'm not some kind of doll to be played with." She growled at him, and he laughed.

"You're my toy to play with. I promise you'll be screaming my name in a good way very soon." He pressed a thumb to her clit and stared at his hand in the mirror. Two fingers were inside her body, and his thumb stroked from side to side. "I'm going to fuck you very soon, but before I do, you're going to tell me who you belong to."

He wasn't letting up this time. Murphy had already had one orgasm, and he could wait a hell of a lot longer for a second.

With his free hand, he cupped her breast, thumbing the nipple of one breast. Leaving her breast, he moved her hair off her neck and kissed her. He nibbled on her neck, going round to her collar bone.

She whimpered in response.

Going along the back of her neck, he moved her hair to the other side to give her neck on the opposite side the same attention.

"All you've got to do is say the words." When she was close to climaxing, he withdrew his hand, letting her calm down before touching her again.

"Not fair. Not fair. Not fair," she said.

"You know who I am, Tate. I'll take everything you can fire at me, but at the end of the day, I won't be going anywhere. You can think this is going to be our one and only time, but you're very much mistaken. This is our first time of many. You can push me away, curse me, hit me, even deny me everything. You and I both know you belong to me, and you have done since prom night. I laid claim to you then, and I'll keep doing it for a long time to come. There's no getting away from me. I'm here to stay, and you're going to have to accept that."

He turned her head and claimed her lips with his own. She moaned, whimpering against his mouth. Murphy didn't stop. Plunging his tongue in deep, he fucked her mouth like he was going to fuck her cunt.

There was no letting up. He'd made up his mind. Tate was going to fight him every step of the way when they got back to Fort Wills, and he was going to fight back. He looked forward to showing her how much he loved her.

When she was eighteen, she'd promised to love him, to be there for him. It was time for Tate to realize she should never make that kind of promise to him lightly.

"I'm yours, I belong to you, only you," she said.

Murphy stroked her clit and sank three fingers into her pussy. He brought her to orgasm within seconds, and he watched her climax in the mirror. Her cunt tightened around his fingers, soaking them with her cream. He didn't mind her wet heat.

When she was finished, he lifted her off his lap, aligned his cock to her entrance and slammed inside bringing her back onto his lap again.

"Watch us together, Tate. See what you do to me." In the mirror it was clear to see his cock inside her body. "Nothing else has been inside you apart from a fake rubber cock. I'm not fake, baby. I'm warm, hard, male, and I'm not letting you use anything else to be inside you again. This is all mine."

"Yes!"

He fucked her hard, bending her in front and riding her deep from behind. Murphy slapped her ass and pressed a finger into her ass, stretching her out. He was going to take her ass very soon.

She screamed, crying out, and she gripped him tight. Closing his eyes, Murphy let out a roar as he jerked inside her, climaxing for a second time. Her body shook under his. Caressing her back, Murphy didn't want to leave the welcoming warmth of her body.

"I can't move," she said. Her voice shook.

Withdrawing from her body, he picked her up in his arms. He was too exhausted for a shower and dropped them both to the bed.

"Shouldn't we wash first?" she asked.

"Tomorrow, we can worry about everything else tomorrow." Murphy settled in beside her, rubbing her stomach as he got comfortable.

The silence stretched between them. "We've got to talk properly about what happened," he said, broaching the subject that was still between them. She tensed in his arms, shutting him out.

"There's nothing to talk about," she said, obviously bluffing him.

"We both know that's not the case. You can't keep doing this to me, Tate."

She rolled over, looking him in the eye. "I've just fucked you twice, Murphy. Twice I let you inside my body when I promised myself I'd never let you near me. I'm not doing anything. Just back off with everything else, and don't spoil tonight." She turned away, settling down in the bed.

"Fine. I'll let it drop for tonight, but tomorrow we're talking about this, whether you like it or not."

"Fine!" she said, getting the last word in.

Holding her close, Murphy listened to her even breathing and waited for her to fall asleep before he drifted into sleep himself.

****

Tate opened her eyes and stared at the wall opposite the bed. Murphy's arm was banded around her waist making it difficult to move. Looking up at the clock she saw it was a little after six. She glanced behind her to see him deep in sleep. Her past experience with him let her know he was so deep in sleep he wouldn't easily wake.

Wiggling out from under his arm, Tate made her way off the bed, replacing her frame with several pillows for him to hold. Without looking at him, she made her way into the bathroom. She did her business quickly and knew she didn't have time to shower or anything else.

Her body was sticky from the sauce and cream last time. Pouting, she left the room and grabbed some clothes from the wardrobe being as careful as possible. When he didn't make a sound she tip-toed out of the hotel room. At the same time she closed her door she heard two more doors closing.

Kelsey and Eva were coming out of two separate rooms. Her friend looked a little dazed while Eva appeared to be in the same condition as Tate. Had her father taken Eva last night?

Eva glanced up at her and then quickly averted her gaze. *Well holy crap.* All three women headed to the elevator at the same time. None spoke until the doors closed.

"I didn't do anything with Killer. He sat up most of the night watching porn. He barely spoke to me," Kelsey said, tucking some hair behind her ear.

"I fucked Murphy," Tate said, breaking through the small silence that had settled since Kelsey spoke. Eva glanced at her.

"Are you all right?" Eva asked.

"You slept with my father. It's gross, disgusting, but I know you love him. Does it change things between the two of you?"

The older woman laughed. "Changes things? No, it only highlights to me that I need to move on. Tiny is never going to let me in his life. He's got the ghost of your mother, no offence. I'm not going to stick around for the aftermath of everything. You're a grown woman, Tate. It's time for me to move out and move on."

They were not the words she'd been hoping to hear.

"Dad's hard, Eva. You know this. Give him time."

"Time? Honey, Tiny is nothing like Murphy. I know you've got your problems with him, but they're two different men. I bet your man didn't tell you sleeping with you was a huge mistake and it was one he won't be repeating," Eva said, slamming her hand over her mouth seconds later.

"He said that?" Tate was shocked by her father. She knew he was a hard nut, but she also knew he had feelings for Eva. Her nanny was the only woman Tiny had gotten close to since her mother died, and he was always fucking it up.

"Yes. I'm serious, Tate. I'm done. This weekend has been the best and worst of my life. I'm moving out the moment we get back."

"You can move in with me," Tate said. She'd love the company.

"No. I've been looking into a place for some time. I don't need your help to get on my feet."

The elevator doors opened to reveal her uncle stood waiting.

"Eva," Alex said.

"Fuck off." She didn't give Alex a chance to finish as Eva stormed away. "I'll give you five minutes, Tate, and then we're leaving."

Kelsey followed Eva out of the building.

"Rough night?" Alex asked.

"It has been a rough couple of years." Tate stared at her uncle wondering what he could want. She wasn't interested in what he had to say, but seeing as he was her uncle, she wanted to give him the benefit of the doubt.

"I'm sorry about last night," he said.

"Which part? Giving my dad rooms for the night or letting them spoil our weekend? The three of us were going to have a girly weekend, and it turned out a disaster. Tiny has fucked everything up with Eva, and Kelsey, my one friend, probably won't be talking to me for a long time." Tate shook her head. "Look, I guess you're a great guy because you're my mother's brother, but I don't know you and to be honest, I don't want to get to know you," Tate said, meaning it.

"I've wanted to get to know *you* for a long time. The club—"

"Always comes first. I know. I've been living the club coming first all my life. There's nothing new about it. Dad puts the club first. Murphy puts the club first, and as usual I get pushed aside. I know that may sound selfish to you, but living in the shadows of a brotherhood kind of sucks." Tate brushed past him feeling guilty for hating something that had done good even mixed with all the bad. The Skulls was a brotherhood. They were a family, and Fort Wills was a better place for it. Blinking away the tears, Tate kept walking until Alex caught her arm.

She looked up at him, and then his arms were around her, hugging her.

"I love you, Tate. There's always a place for you here. I'll take care of you and look after you. You'll want for nothing."

Tate nodded and pulled away. She ran out toward the taxi waiting for them. Eva was sat in the front seat as Kelsey sat in the back.

"Did you change our plane tickets?" Tate asked. She wiped at the tears gathering in her eyes.

"Yes, I did it from his room."

"What about our clothes?" Kelsey said. "I didn't even think about the clothes I was leaving behind."

"Don't worry about it. The guys will bring them back," Eva said. "They're good like that. Keeping everyone at arms' length but seeming like sweet guys."

None of them spoke as the driver cleared his throat. Talking club business in front of him wasn't a good idea. Closing her mouth, Tate went to looking out of her window. Her thoughts were focused on the night she'd spent with Murphy.

She cursed her own foolishness as her pussy tightened with each memory. One night was never going to be enough with him, and thinking it would was a big mistake on her part.

At the airport, Eva paid the driver, and they climbed out. When they were at the desk, Tate let Eva take charge. She noticed Eva's hands were shaking, and she recognized the tell-tale signs of the other woman's distress.

"We're in different areas of the plane. Tate, you're with Kelsey."

"You did that on purpose," Tate said, glaring at her.

Eva glanced up. "I want to be alone, Tate. This is nothing to do with you."

"I'm here for you. He's my father—"

"Exactly, he's your father. I'm not going to come between you two. Last night I realized that no matter how much you wish and hope, your dreams don't always come true." Eva shrugged. "My heart was ripped out, but at least I know where I stand."

She watched Eva walk away.

"Our plane is scheduled for take-off in thirty minutes," Kelsey said.

Tate went through the motions of boarding a plane. Her insides were in knots, and she felt guilty every time she looked toward Eva. On the plane, Eva was not in sight. Taking her seat, she took the window seat so Kelsey didn't have to look out of it.

"Thank you," Kelsey said.

"No problems. You've got a fear of heights, and I'm fine with it." Tate sat back, closing her eyes, trying to catch her breath.

Once they were in the sky, Tate finally relaxed.

"There's a lot of history between you and Eva?" Kelsey asked.

"She used to be my nanny. I'm sure you've heard all the gossip. I'm twenty-four, and my father decided to get me a nanny five years older than me. It's ridiculous." Tate shook her head, feeling the beginnings of a headache.

"Or he's really smart."

Glancing over at her new friend, Tate frowned. "What do you mean?"

"Well, he picked someone you wouldn't think he was replacing your mother with or be too strict on you. He chose a woman who was near your age but responsible. I think your father was looking out for you in his choice." Kelsey took a soda from the woman with the tray of food. Tate asked for some peanuts as well.

"Did I mention he's been wanting Eva for a long time in his bed? You know, fucking and doing all kinds of nasty," Tate said.

Kelsey winced. "I'm never going to get used to your language."

"I've grew up with men always talking like that. It's natural to me, and I don't do it to be hard on you. It's who I am."

"I'm not complaining. My family is a little different. I've learned to accept them and their way of dealing with things. They have a cuss jar that you have to pay a fine. Also, they had a naughty step. I know, strange right, but they had one." Kelsey laughed. "They're good parents."

"They sound like it." Tate didn't grow up with a cuss jar. Thinking back to her childhood, she remembered the barbeques her mother always organized for the guys. Tate used to be passed around the bikers, and they all treated her like a daughter. Lash and Nash, or Nigel and Edward, were always there as well.

She couldn't argue with the way her father had brought her up.

"Anyway, maybe you should give your father the benefit of the doubt."

"Yeah, I'm sure Tiny's full of the affection and tender loving care."

"Tiny? Is that your father's name?" Kelsey asked.

"No," Tate said, laughing. "His real name is Maximus Johnson."

Kelsey joined in laughing with her. It was fun to get back to laughing again. It felt like a lifetime ago since she'd just let loose and laughed.

"So, what happened with you and the new guy?" Tate asked, cutting through the laughter as they were gaining attention.

"Nothing. He didn't talk to me." Kelsey fidgeted in her seat. "He stared at me a lot. It was weird."

"Maybe he wanted to get his freak on with you."

Her friend went bright red. "I doubt that. I'm not exactly biker material."

Tate scoffed. "Honey, I'm not biker material, and yet I had my legs wrapped around a biker last night."

"It's different for you. You grew up with it. I'm not used to such attention. His gaze was dark, and it was like he was undressing me. I know, undressing the fat whale," Kelsey said.

She glared at her friend. "Don't talk about yourself like that. You're a beautiful woman, Kelsey, and never let anyone tell you differently."

Tate gasped as she was transported back to when she was seventeen. Several of the girls in high school had been picking on her, calling her names and making jokes at her clothes. None of them ever spoke to her when Murphy was around. They still liked to invite her to parties, but they were never nice when they didn't have to be. He was the one who kept them all quiet. In fact, she'd gotten a lot more invites to parties once she was seen around with him.

Unable to face any more jokes or name calling she'd hidden out at the back of the gym where no one went. She'd been sat with her knees up against her chest when Murphy found her.

He'd sat down beside and listened to everything she had to say. How had she forgotten the way he touched her face and brought her close to him?

"Listen to me, Tate, you're a beautiful woman. Those girls are jealous because you're the type of woman a man wants. When you're older you're going to meet the right man to settle down with while they're being passed from man to man. Don't let anyone tell you differently."

She'd completely forgotten about that.

Chapter Seven

"Tate?" Murphy called her name a third time and knew she'd gone. Checking out the wardrobe he saw her clothes were still there along with Eva's and Cherry's. "Fuck!" Tiny was going to kill him.

The next time he saw Tate she was going over his knee. He didn't care if she didn't talk to him for a week. There was no way he was going to accept his woman running out on him.

Pulling on his jeans and shirt, Murphy grabbed his jacket and headed out of the hotel room. He found Tiny and the rest of the guys at the bar eating breakfast. Alex was with them as well.

Lash and Angel were sat together giggling.

"Will you two shut the fuck up?" Nash asked, groaning. Murphy saw one side of Nash's face was a nice shade of purple.

"Have you heard the good news?" Lash asked, ignoring his brother.

Taking a seat Murphy waited to be updated.

"We got married last night," Angel said, showing the men her ring. They all gave her encouraging comments and smiled, admiring the ring. Nash even smiled at her.

"Don't worry, I know Tate's gone," Tiny said, drawing Murphy back to him.

"They left early this morning," Alex said.

"Did they say anything to you?" Murphy grabbed himself a plate of food and started eating. Tate's scent still surrounded him. He'd not gotten in the shower or washed their time away.

"Not worth repeating." Alex was clicking away on the computer, clearly bored with talking.

"What happened with Eva last night?" he asked.

"A fat lot of nothing." Tiny slammed his cup down. "We're leaving after breakfast. They have a lead on us, and I'm pissed off. Don't talk to me. Pack their shit up and meet me down in the lobby in thirty minutes."

Tiny stormed away.

"He fucked Eva last night and fucked things up," Nash said. "I'll be surprised if she doesn't leave his ass."

"She's been threatening to leave him for some time, Nash. It's not going to happen," Lash said.

"Tate's no longer living with him. There's no reason for Eva to stay. Why would she stay around for someone who didn't want her?"

Murphy finished his breakfast refusing to be drawn into another debate about the Tiny and Eva drama. He remembered it coming from Tate when she was younger. She'd always wanted the two to get together. Over the years, the club had just grown bored with the same old shit. He figured Tiny would be inside a sweet-butt within a matter of minutes from the moment they got home.

"I'm going to clear their shit away," Murphy said, leaving them to their argument.

"I'll come as well." Killer followed him upstairs to the main hotel room where the women should be staying. Going through to the bedroom, Murphy noted Killer's glance at the rumpled bed.

"Keep your fucking opinions to yourself," Murphy said.

"I'm not saying anything. I spent the whole night watching porn while Cherry stared at me. We didn't speak one word." Killer moved to the wardrobe and started pulling clothes out.

"You don't live up to your name, do you?" Murphy asked.

"I kill people with my bare hands. I live up to my name. I've had no reason to kill recently. The Skulls have never killed for sport whereas The Lions loved it." Killer's voice held no emotion. The other man was hard and dead to the world.

Murphy knew the tales and hated the fact anyone had to go through what The Lions had put Killer through. He was a good guy inside, but the deceased leader of the other club had killed everything else.

"The first time they told me to kill someone I did it without hesitation. There was this guy in the middle of the warehouse. He'd been badly beaten and had done some wrong to the club. My loyalty was to my club, to my brothers. The man was a threat, and I ended him." Killer's gaze appeared off into the distance, to a past time that was not right now. Murphy waited, knowing patience was best. "Do you know what the guy had done?"

Shaking his head, Murphy folded his arms waiting to be given the crap news.

"The guy had denied the club access to his wife. The wife was a small, beautiful woman and had caught the club's eye." Killer shook his head. "I killed a man because my leader wanted to fuck someone else's wife."

Going to him, Murphy put a hand on his shoulder. "We all do shit for our clubs that feels right."

"You betrayed your club to infiltrate mine. I'm thankful you did. The Lions were a fucking curse, but still, betraying your brothers had to be hard."

He looked away. "My brothers knew what I was doing. I didn't betray the club. They acted like I did. The real betrayal is with Tate. I fucked up. I promised her shit, and I didn't deliver. She doesn't give a shit about what happened at the club. Tate cares about what I did to her."

"Tiny's daughter?" Killer asked.

Sitting on the edge of the bed, Murphy let out a sigh. He pulled out his packet of cigarettes and lit one. "My first job as a prospect was babysitting duty. Fucking hated it. I was better than that. I was too good for babysitting my leader's daughter." Murphy took a long drag of his cigarette.

"Was she a bitch?"

"No, not at all. Tate was nothing like she is now. She was sweet, charming, and the most amazing person I'd ever known." Licking his lips, Murphy offered Killer a cigarette. "It didn't take long until the best part of my life was being with her. I pretended to the guys how much I hated it, but I loved it. She was sunshine in our dark world. Tate didn't judge, and she never accused me of anything. It was nice to sit with her, listen to her talk and talk about everything."

"You fell in love with her?" Killer asked, taking a seat and lighting up his cigarette.

"I fell in love with her. On prom night, I was her date. I kissed her, and I had every intention of telling her my feelings. I told her how I felt even though I'd decided in the same night, not to. She was in my arms, and I couldn't imagine being anywhere else but with her. We were going to fuck or at least, she wanted to. She was ready. I was an idiot and not ready for that. I wanted to talk with her father and take my time. Not every girl should lose their virginity prom night." Murphy shook his head at the stupidity of his actions. "I promised her commitment. I promised her that she'd always come first, and then the job of infiltrating The Lions came up. I'd earned my patch by then and was ready to help the club. They needed someone who could go inside, gather information without any problems. There was a plan, and I volunteered for the job."

"What about Tate?"

"The club came first, and I broke my promise. You knew what I was like, Killer. I fucked any woman I wanted. I was a monster. "

"What are your thoughts now?" Killer asked.

"I've got to win her back. For the past couple of years I've stood back and watched her grieve and change. I can't let her go, Killer."

They were silent as they finished their smokes.

"How come you don't feel betrayed by me?" Murphy asked, getting up.

"You didn't turn your back on the club, Murphy. I wasn't there when the shooting went down, but I knew you'd be the kind of person I'd want to be joined with. The Skulls are bastards, and yet, there's a sense of friendship and support. You don't turn on each other. I want that."

Killer grabbed the clothes, and they headed down to the lobby.

Angel and Lash were wrapped around each other, kissing and making a spectacle of themselves.

The drive to the airport was tense. The only sounds were Lash's moans and Angel's giggles, which were driving him insane.

When they hit the earth after the long flight back home, Murphy was anxious to get to Tate's house.

"I'm going home. Bring Tate back home tomorrow," Tiny said, leaving him to handle everything. The airport housed their bikes. It had cost a pretty penny, but it was worth it.

Climbing on his bike he noticed Killer follow him as he neared the apartment building where Tate lived. Stopping into a lay-by he waited for Killer to catch up with him.

"What are you doing, man? Tate's going to be fighting me. You don't want to see that."

"I was going to give Cherry back her clothes. She deserves to have them back after we ruined their weekend."

Nodding, Murphy gave the other man a bag. "I'll get her apartment number for you to give the clothes back."

They were riding toward the apartment building once again. With every mile they drove Murphy was tensing up ready for a fight. Tate was different, and he knew she was going to fight him every step of the way. He couldn't lose sight of what he wanted.

The Tate she'd once been was still in there. He was the one responsible for ruining everything for her.

Parking the bike in the first available space he waited for Killer to do the same. "Go to the front door. I'll text you the number."

"Where are you going?" Killer asked.

"I always surprise my girl."

Going around the back of the building, Murphy found the ledge he needed to start climbing the building. The first time he'd climbed into her bedroom window, Tate hadn't been able to stop laughing at his gesture. He'd showed her it was lame and clichéd for a guy to sneak into a woman's bedroom window. What Tate didn't know was he'd gotten Eva's help to do it. She kept Tiny occupied while he gave Tate what she always wanted.

Climbing up the building Murphy cursed his efforts. "Fucking killed men and wasting my time making shit special for my woman. Bad fucking form. I should just use my dick instead."

Her window was partially open.

"If you're trying to make women go crazy then stop ranting at yourself," Tate said. She was stood facing the window with her arms folded.

"How the fuck did you know I was coming?" he asked, closing the window behind him.

"I heard the bikes and saw you heading toward the back. You're a creature of habit, Murphy. The window? You've told me loads of times before how fucking lame it is."

She left the bedroom, and he went after her. He was struck by the curves of her ass, and his cock thickened. Fuck, he needed to get inside her again very soon. He was going to lose his mind.

"My guy is downstairs. He's got Cherry's clothes for her."

"Her name is Kelsey. Okay, K.E.L.S.E.Y. That's her name, not Cherry, not tubby, but Kelsey."

"Okay, Killer's got Kelsey's clothes for her."

"Killer? Seriously, you've got a killer with my friend." She shoved him hard. He grabbed her arms stopping her from pushing him away.

"I get it. You don't want me calling your friend by any other name. Give me her number, and I promise you he won't hurt her."

"She's not part of the club, Murphy."

Murphy agreed. Tate gave him the room number. He sent the text to Killer and got the response that he was there.

Turning his cell off, he threw the device on the coffee table. He found Tate in the kitchen, making a hot chocolate. The scent of cinnamon, milk, and chocolate filled the air. It was her mother's recipe. He knew because she'd told him about it.

"Does Tiny know Eva's leaving?" Tate asked.

"She won't leave."

He moved up behind her, wrapping his arms around her waist. She was so soft. Burying his head in her neck, Murphy groaned. She smelt so good.

"Then you're all going to be shocked because she's leaving him." Tate didn't pull away from him.

"Why did you run this morning?" he asked. He searched for the sash of the robe and started to untie it. Her hands covered his.

"What happens in Vegas stays in Vegas. This, us, is staying there."

He tugged on the sash releasing her robe. "I don't think so."

****

Why was he being difficult? They were never going to work together, and he was only going to make it worse. Not to mention what her father was going to do when he realized the truth. Tiny had known about her feelings, but he'd never known how far things had gotten.

His hand touched her bare stomach, and she gasped, sucking her stomach in.

"You shouldn't be doing this," she said, trying to find ways to stop him.

Don't stop him. I want his touch so damn much.

She was drowning with her need for him. From the sight of him coming through her bedroom window she'd been ready for him. His long hair, wide shoulders, and impressive cock was all it took to make her horny. She'd never been the type of woman to be controlled by her hormones. Murphy was her only exception.

"No, we should be doing this. Our mistake was waiting this long to do this." He nibbled on the lobe of her ear. She squealed as his tongue pressed inside.

"You left to fuck your whores, Murphy. This is over."

"Are you sure about that?" Murphy asked.

She spun around facing him and gasped as he pushed the robe to the floor. He lifted her up onto the counter, spreading her thighs wide.

Tate wondered how he moved so fast. One moment she'd been dressed, and now she was waiting for his cock.

She watched him push his jeans to the floor and grip his cock in one hand. Within seconds he was inside her. Tate moaned, feeling him stretch her inch by glorious inch as he sank to the hilt.

"That's it, baby, squeeze my dick. Let me feel all of you." He sucked on her nipple at the same time he gripped her ass, plunging inside. "So fucking tight. Perfect tits, perfect pussy."

"We need to stop," she said, moaning.

"No, we're doing this all the time. You're not turning me away or pushing me away. We're in this together, Tate." He slammed into her, gripping her neck and claiming her lips.

He was everywhere. She held onto his jacket as he drew her away from the counter. Squealing, Tate held on. He shoved her against the fridge. "Been thinking about fucking you since I woke up. I was going to lick your sweet cunt until you came on my face, and then you went and spoilt the surprise by leaving. I'm going to have to make it up to you now."

She shook her head. "No, this has to be the last time. We can't keep doing this. I hate you."

"You pussy is dripping, Tate. You're not hating me right now."

"I am." She hated the sound of her own voice. The bastard was right. Tate was holding him close not wanting to let go of him.

"Well, if this is what you feel like when you're hating me, I can't wait to see what you're like when you're loving me."

He slammed his lips down on hers cutting off her retort. Wrapping her arms around his neck, Tate moaned. She held him close not wanting to let go.

"Fuck me," she said, begging him. His jeans were around his ankles, but she didn't care. All she cared about was how deep he could be inside her.

Pushing his leather jacket to the floor, she tore at his shirt until his tattooed chest was naked.

"That's it, baby. Touch me."

She scored his back with her nails as he fucked her hard against the fridge. They were both panting, crying out for more.

He moved away from the fridge once again. Tate squealed, hating how easily he could move her. She was used to being too big for someone to pick up. Murphy must really be into the weights.

"Where are you going?" she asked, moaning as his cock hit a spot right deep.

"Bedroom."

Once inside he tossed her to the bed. His cock left her pussy. She sat up on the bed and watched him go to her drawers. Murphy opened the top drawer and pulled out her smallest dildo.

"What are you doing?" she asked, pushing hair out of her eyes.

"We're going to have a little fun."

He joined her back on the bed carrying some lube and her dildo.

"Suck it," he said, presenting the tip of the dildo to her lips. Staring at him, she opened her mouth and sucked the cock into her mouth.

She felt a spasm deep in her cunt as his eyes went a shade darker. "Fuck, so sexy."

Smiling, she bobbed her head on the dildo loving the way his own cock jerked in reaction. Tate moaned soaking the shaft with her saliva.

"Enough," he said, tearing the length from her lips. He ran his fingers over her lips and smiled. "Such sinful lips. They look beautiful wrapped around my dick."

Tate licked his fingers, teasing him some more.

"Not today. Got on your hands and knees and kneel."

Rolling her eyes at his order she knelt on the bed presenting him with her ass. His hands went to her hips.

She cried out as with one harsh thrust, he slammed inside her, taking her by surprise with his possession.

"That's right, baby. Feel who owns you." For good measure he plunged into her three more times making her cry out. "My pussy. My tits and my woman. You're all mine," Murphy said.

Yes.

Tate didn't say the words aloud. She wouldn't give him the satisfaction.

Something cool worked at her anus. Gasping, Tate tried to pull away, but Murphy wouldn't let her. With one grip on her hip, he held her in place as the thing at her ass opened her up.

"Take what I'm giving you," he said.

"Don't, Murphy." Even as she spoke the words she moaned.

"You've never had a real cock here, but I know this dildo was not for anything other than your ass. You better have cleaned them the last time you used them."

Tate glared at him over her shoulder. "With boiling water, which is exactly what I'm going to do with your cock. You fucking whore."

He growled and slapped her ass. “Be careful, baby. You’re threatening to turn me on.” Murphy slapped her ass again and again until she was begging him to stop. Throughout it all he’d worked the tip of the dildo into her ass.

She moaned, pushing back against him.

“There we go, baby. See, you like getting your ass fucked. Take a deep breath, and push out for me.”

His sarcastic tone was going to get him killed very soon.

Murphy pressed the cock into her ass, slamming his own cock into her pussy at the same time.

The burn along with the pleasure made for a heady combination. Closing her eyes, she dropped her head in her hands as he worked her body. Murphy knew exactly what to do to push her to the edge of pleasure without throwing her over into bliss.

The dildo in her ass worked in time with the cock in her pussy. Each one totally different from each other but designed to give her the exact same thing, release.

His hand moved from her hip to reach between her thighs. Two fingers teased her clit, drawing her need out further. She whimpered, begging him to stop.

“I want you to come, Tate. Let me feel you come around my cock.”

Biting down on her lip, Tate tried to hold off her orgasm, but it was too much. Murphy hurtled her over the edge into the most delicious ecstasy, one that she didn’t want to come down from.

She heard his growl of completion and felt it deep in her womb as his release left his cock, coating her.

He removed the dildo from her ass but left his cock inside her as they collapsed to the bed. His arms circled her waist holding her close.

“You shouldn’t have come tonight,” Tate said.

"It's not like you gave me much choice. You were gone this morning. I missed you." He kissed her neck, and all she wanted to do was sink against him.

Letting out a sigh, Tate looked across her room at the plain white walls. "What happens in Vegas—"

"Shut the fuck up about that. Shit like that doesn't work with us. Did you know Lash and Angel got married there this weekend?" Murphy asked.

Glancing behind her, Tate stared at him. "What?"

"Seriously, Angel and Lash are husband and wife."

"I thought they were having a big wedding?"

"They couldn't wait." Murphy pushed her hair out of the way to kiss her neck.

"I was supposed to be a bridesmaid."

He licked her neck, nibbling on her ear.

"Angel didn't say anything, but she was a little upset you didn't invite her to Vegas with you and Eva. You invited a girl you've only just met instead of Angel." His hand stroked up and down her hip.

"Kelsey's nice. She's different."

"Different, how?" he asked.

"She's not involved in the club. Angel is Lash's woman. She's part of that world. I don't want to be part of that world anymore."

"You're Tiny's daughter. It makes it part of your world. Besides, you're my woman, and I'm part of the club."

Tate shook her head. "No, we're having sex. This is not part of anything other than a bit of fun." She felt him tense behind her.

"A bit of fun?" he asked.

"Yeah. I'm not serious about you, Murphy. I could never trust you. You fuck everything that walks."

Her words were a lie, but she said them anyway.

"Say what you want, Tate. I know the truth. I know the real you even if you do try to hide it from everyone else."

Tears were so close to the surface. Tate batted them away. Tears were not useful. They were a pain in the ass, and she would only end up hurt by them

He pressed a hand to her stomach. "Anyway, I'm not going anywhere because you could be pregnant. I've not been wearing a rubber, and last time I checked you weren't taking any precautions either."

Tate jerked. She tugged out of his arms and stared down at him, pressing a hand to her stomach. No, it couldn't be, but she knew he spoke the truth. They'd had sex multiple times without him wearing anything.

How could she have been so stupid?

Chapter Eight

"You stupid fucking bastard." Tate threw a pillow at him and stormed out of the room. Her face was bright red. Murphy checked her ass out as she walked out. She looked so fucking sexy. His cock hardened at the thought of her pregnant with his child. He'd love for her to have a boy and a girl. Murphy didn't care which as long as they were healthy and looked like him and Tate.

Hearing dishes and pans crashing about in the other room, Murphy followed her through to the kitchen. She was moving shit around. He'd seen her do this growing up when she had an argument with her father.

"Tate, what are you doing?" he asked. Checking the time he saw it was a little after ten. If she didn't be quiet the neighbors would complain, which would mean more shit for him.

"I fucking hate you. I hope your dick falls off." She charged toward him, poking him in the chest as she spoke. "No, I hope you get some disease that rots your dick off and you can't have any sex, ever."

He caught her hand, pulling her close. "Why are you so angry?"

"Pregnant? Murphy, I don't want to have kids with you. I didn't even want to sleep with you let alone keep up a relationship with you."

Her words stung.

"There was a time when you loved me," he said. "You wanted me, and you wanted this."

Wrapping an arm around her back, Murphy stared down into her glistening eyes. She looked so lost and scared.

Her lip quivered. "I wanted everything with you, Murphy. I wanted the big house with the white picket fence and the shitty neighbors who gossiped behind our backs." She stopped to take a breath. "I thought we'd have a house full of kids, boys and girls. We'd get married, and everything would be perfect."

"Everything can be perfect. We can have those things, Tate."

She shook her head. "No, we can't because I wanted all of those things, and then you went and joined The Lions. You put the club first, and I get that."

His heart ached as he knew what was coming next. He didn't want to hear the rest of her words. Murphy wanted her to be quiet as he knew he'd hurt her deeply.

"I saw you around the mall, and even before that I saw you with them."

"What are you talking about? I saw you at the mall, and I kept my distance," Murphy said. He'd done everything to keep her safe and away from the shit that was going on.

"When Dad told me what was going on and that you'd left to go to The Lions. I didn't believe him. I went to your cabin out by the lake to see for myself. The one you said you only went to in order to think." The tears she'd been holding in were dripping down her face. "I was stood behind a tree, and I saw you all. I heard you as well."

He felt sick to his stomach. The cabin had been the place he'd started his initiation into The Lions. They'd started to hang out there. He'd since gutted the place and intended to do it all up.

"What did you hear and see?" he asked.

"I heard you telling them about me, Murphy. Laughing at how you got me to fall in love with you. I was just some sport for you to play with."

Murphy cupped her cheeks. "Stop, that wasn't the real me. I did what I had to for the club. You think I liked doing that? Do you think I liked talking about you in that way?" He stroked her cheek. "I hated every second of my time with them. All I wanted to do was be with you."

"You chose the club."

"I chose to protect you, Tate. I didn't choose the club."

"You left me all alone. I was confused, and you'd promised me forever. What do you want from me, Murphy? What more do you want to take? I can't be the person you want. I'm not cut out to be an old lady."

He tilted her head back and claimed her lips. "I'm going to go for tonight. I need you to calm down, and I've got some thinking to do. I'll be back." Murphy kissed her again. "I love you."

Turning away, Murphy walked out of her apartment and went straight for his bike. He saw Killer's bike was still there in the parking lot. Murphy didn't bother going back to talk to him or seeing what the other guy was doing. It wasn't his place, and he needed to get away from the shit that was going on in his own life.

Straddling his bike, he drove toward the cabin. He'd not been back to this place since the shooting in Tiny's place. With the wind in his face, Murphy remembered the look of fear on Tate's face as she'd looked at him. She'd been terrified of him because she knew what he was capable of.

"Are you happy now?" Tate asked.

She'd stared at him the whole time. He'd wanted to tell her that he was on her side, but he couldn't. The only thing he could do was keep his mouth shut and hope Tiny and his men got there in time.

"Is this what you wanted, death? No wonder you wanted to go with the Lions, they're just fucking pigs in a jacket," Tate said.

He'd kept his shit together when Jeff backhanded her, but it was he who ended that scum's life. No one touched his woman and got away with it. During his years inside The Lions he'd taken out all the men who'd said a bad word. No one suspected it was him. Any who suggested kidnapping or hurting Tate in any way and Murphy made sure to put an end to them.

There had been so many dead bodies, and he'd hidden them all. When it was safe he'd phoned Tiny letting him know what was happening.

No one hurt Tate. She was the one thing that was good in his world, and he'd be damned if he was going to let someone destroy it. It was not happening, not on his watch.

At the driveway of the cabin, he phoned Tiny to let him know where he was. His leader didn't say a word and asked about Tate. Murphy gave an update, closed the cell phone, and turned it off. He didn't want to be disturbed.

He climbed off his bike and headed into the cabin. It wasn't really a cabin, but his folks always spoke of it as a cabin as it was the place they used to go to in order to get away. Going to the fridge, he grabbed the six pack of beer and headed out. The chairs were all neatly folded. He unfolded one and sat down. The cool beer helped to parch his thirst. Staring out across the lake, Murphy remembered the night Tate was talking about. He knew what she'd seen. After the guys had trashed talked The Skulls, they'd turned on Tate, Tiny's daughter. They joked about her infatuation. All the time, Murphy had been sick to his stomach as Tate was the one reason he was at The Lions.

She didn't know how big a threat they'd become to Fort Wills. His becoming a member had stopped it, and he'd helped to bring them down. Everything he'd done was to give him and Tate a future.

Sipping his beer, he felt the bitter taste of failure fill him again.

Tate, the one good thing in his life and he'd fucked it up.

The sound of another bike coming in close filled the silence.

Pulling the gun out of his resting place around his ankle, he released the safety and waited. The Lions were still out there. They were a threat that the Skulls were eliminating one by one.

Lash and Nash appeared around the corner. Both looked somber as they headed toward him. He saw they each carried a six pack of beer.

"What are you two doing here?" They were close brothers with Lash being the oldest.

"Angel's on her period and being a bitch," Lash said, grabbing himself a chair.

"Kate's nowhere to be seen, and the sweet-butts are pissing me off." Nash took a chair and sat off to the side of him.

"Tiny told us where you were, and we figured you could use some company. Male company only." Lash pulled the cap off the bottle and sat down.

"What my brother doesn't tell you is Eva's moved out without a word and Tiny's being an ass," Nash said, doing the same as his brother with his beer.

"It's been a long couple of days," Murphy said.

"I haven't been up here in years." Lash sat back, sighing. "I love coming here."

"I'm in love with Tate, and I may or may not have gotten her pregnant," Murphy said, needing to talk to someone.

Nash spit out the beer he'd been drinking as Lash glared at him.

"Tiny's going to kick your ass."

"She won't give me the time of day. Tate talks about my time with The Lions. The shit I had to do and she's got no idea at all." He sipped his bottle, wishing it was something stronger.

"You're going to accept the beating her father's going to give you?" Nash asked.

"Yeah, I'll do anything for Tate. She's always been my number one priority."

"Even though you fucked a load of women when you decided to be a spy?" Nash was the only one talking.

Glancing over at Lash, Murphy saw the other man deep in thought. "You didn't become a spy for The Skulls. You became a spy for Tate."

"They were the threat of the town and to The Skulls. Tate never deserved to live in fear. She always deserved happiness and love. I always wanted that for her."

"You sound like a pussy," Nash said. "Actually, you sound like my brother, Nigel." He smirked at Lash. Murphy rolled his eyes. These two were fucking idiots when they started.

"Forget I ever said anything," Murphy said.

"No, we're men here. Hey, Edward, why don't you tell Dillon that you've got a hard on for Kate's younger sister?"

The smile on Nash's face disappeared. "You're an asshole."

"Yeah, I'm your asshole brother."

"You've got the hots for Kate's younger sister?" Murphy asked. "I didn't even realize Kate had a sister."

"She doesn't come to the club. Getting into the pants of a Skull is not her main priority."

Murphy didn't push it. He was in love with the daughter of a man who could kill him and dispose of his body easily.

"Tate will come around. She just needs to know what you did and why you did it."

"Also, don't fuck any more pussy. Tate's not the kind of girl to share." Nash added the last bit.

None of their advice helped.

A cell phone went off. Murphy ignored it. He'd shut his cell phone off so he wouldn't be disturbed.

"Fuck, we've got to round the troops together," Lash said.

"What? Why?" Nash asked.

"Tomorrow we're on lockdown. Two of the finest and brightest have just been killed on the outskirts of Fort Wills. The Lions have been sighted. Tiny wants us to put out the word."

****

Tate rubbed at her temple. The phones were ringing constantly, and she was getting tired of saying the same old crap to the same people. That morning she had to deal with a phone call from her father and then an appearance from Murphy. The whole club was going on lockdown, and they wanted her to report to the club. She didn't have anything to do with The Skulls. They didn't need her for lockdown.

"You seem a little distracted today," Kelsey said, sitting in the only available reception chair.

"It's these phones. Everyone's got an issue, and I'm bored." She picked up the phone, holding her finger and asking Kelsey to wait. After booking an appointment for a missing filling, Tate looked back at Kelsey. "The club's on lockdown," she said.

"Lockdown? Oh you mean The Skulls?"

"Yeah, the club. The club my dad runs. You know, the one that keeps this town running smoothly," Tate said. The beginning of a headache began.

"Killer told me a little about it last night," Kelsey said.

"What's going on with you and the newest member of the club?" Tate sat back, looking at her friend. Kelsey's cheeks were a bright red, and she was stuttering as she talked.

"He's, erm, just really nice. I mean, his name is a little terrifying, but everything else about him is kind of awesome. I mean, don't you think?" Kelsey asked.

"I don't know. I've not met Killer. He must be a new guy." Tate stared until Kelsey jumped up out of her seat.

"I need to help with suction."

"I'm sure you do," Tate said, teasing.

"You're not helping me at all."

Tate laughed as Kelsey walked off to go and deal with the suction. She really liked her friend and was pleased she relaxed enough to enjoy her. Glancing at the clock, she saw it was a little after ten.

Several of the women muttered as they walked past. She'd grown used to it and ignored them. Ignoring people was a lot easier and quieter way for her to get through her day. Half an hour later a woman sat in front of her desk, folded her arms and cleared her throat. Looking up, Tate saw Rose, Hardy's wife, the sexy redhead who drove most of the men crazy, all of the men apart from Murphy.

She remembered Murphy didn't attend any of the parties once he'd gotten to know her. He'd stayed with her and Eva at the house. Why was she suddenly remembering all these sweet facts about him?

Focus on the pain. The pain and the hurt and the fact he fucked other women.

"Are you going to ignore me as well?" Rose asked.

"I'm not ignoring you."

"No? Well, you're ignoring Angel, and she's a sweet girl. She doesn't deserve to be ignored by anyone, which just pisses me off." Rose was a hard nut, and the woman knew it.

Closing her eyes, Tate groaned. "I'm working, Rose. Don't you have things to deal with, like Hardy?"

"Oi, bitch, she free to take a break, or do I have to sit here getting my clothes off for her to get out of here?" Rose asked, directing the question at the guy behind her. Tate turned to see one of her bosses.

Dropping her head in her hands, Tate waited to see what he'd say.

"Yes, she can go."

"And she still has a job afterwards?" Rose asked.

"Yeah, sure."

"Good. Get your coat and meet me out front. Don't keep me waiting." Rose stood and walked away. Tate watched the older woman leave. Rose was in her early thirties but had a figure of a woman ten years younger. She liked Rose a lot.

Getting up from her seat, she grabbed her purse and jacket then left. She found Rose leaning up against the building, waiting.

"I thought I was going to have to call Hardy, so I can get all naked. Those uptight assholes looked like they could use a show."

Laughing, Tate looked down at the ground. "I'm pleased you didn't."

"Now that's a shame. The Tate I remember was up for a lot of shit that got interesting." Rose grabbed her arm, and they headed out toward one of the restaurants Fort Wills had. It was a little Italian place that served breakfast, lunch, and dinner.

The maître d' escorted them to their chair. She saw how the man panted after Rose. It must be all that red hair Rose had. A lot of men panted after the other woman.

Taking a seat, Tate looked over the menu, wondering why Rose was coming after her.

"So, let's cut the crap and all the introductions. I've known you a long time. I've known you since you were little. I was with the club since I was eighteen. Hardy was always my guy. He was only my guy at the club. Tell me what shit is happening." Rose opened the menu, but her gaze was focused on Tate.

Swallowing past the lump in her throat, Tate glanced down in front of her.

"Look, you can lie and dodge all you want. I'm not going anywhere, and I don't think you want me to." Rose folded her arms.

"You're six years older than me," Tate said.

"Actually I'm eight years older than you. I'm thirty-two. You've got something going on with Murphy?" Rose asked.

"What? How did you know that?"

"I'm a woman, honey. I'm a woman, and I see the way he looks at you. We all knew you had a thing for him way back then. I don't imagine something like that goes away," Rose said.

They were silent for several moments. Tate took the time to look through the menu. She couldn't find anything she wanted to eat.

"Just get the pancakes or the muffins."

"It's an Italian place. It's a little rude to only order that," Tate said.

"So, order a coffee then."

Laughing, Tate waited for Rose to signal the waiter. They each ordered a coffee and muffin. No one questioned them, but that probably had something to do with the fact Rose had removed her jacket. Hardy's name and The Skulls were inked on Rose's arm, and also she was wearing one of Hardy's jackets.

"Anyone else they'd have complained," Tate said.

"It's one of the perks to being an old lady for a Skull. No one back chats. The club helps everyone in town, even these places."

"I guess."

Rose stared at her for long moments. The older woman's blue eyes made her nervous.

"Why are you staring at me?"

"I'm trying to see what the problem is."

"What do you mean?" Tate asked, confused.

"I need to know what the club did to you for you to turn your back on it." Rose sat back, looking at her.

"The club didn't do anything."

"Really? Look at it from my perspective. You left your father's house, that's fine. You're working in a dental practice, Tate. My God, how boring could you fucking get? Then let's talk about your trip to Vegas and not inviting Angel. Bitch move if ever I heard one. Then the fact you're refusing to have anything to do with the club, your family."

"It's my decision to make," Tate said. "I'm tired of being second best. Everyone picks the club over me. There, I've said it."

Rose groaned, and Tate looked up to see the other woman glaring at her. "Is this some pampered princess shit? Because I'm not in the mood for that. I thought you were better than that."

"Tiny and Murphy all chose the club before me. My mother died with Tiny loving the club more than her."

"You're fucking wrong. That man loved his wife. He loved her so much that he's not even thought of replacing her," Rose said.

"He's fucking everything in sight."

"Men do that a lot, Tate. They deal with their feelings in different ways from us, but he's not replacing her with a wife. Eva's got everything he's looking for, and yet she's gone and left him."

Tate frowned. "Murphy—"

"They're all making our town safer, Tate. Murphy left and spied for The Skulls to make this place safer for you. That man is in love with you, and you're too blind to see it."

"He fucked other women."

"You didn't have any claim over him at all. He did what he had to do before anything progressed between the two of you."

"Is that how you deal with Hardy? When he's going on his long trips with temptation waiting for him on the open road?" Tate asked. She was being a bitch, but she needed Rose to stop.

"Hardy wouldn't dream of fucking another woman," Rose said, leaning forward.

"How can you be so certain?"

"Because I make sure I'm everything he needs. Hardy doesn't want for anything. I'm every fantasy, every desire, and I make sure he feels that every time we're together." Rose leaned back accepting the cup of coffee the waiter brought. "You're club royalty, Tate. The guys love you, and the girls hate you. The old ladies accept you because of who you are. I like you, Tate, but I think you're being stupid." Rose stopped to drink her coffee. “All the guys will be looking out for you. Murphy’s got a lot of shit to get through to be with you. Think about that when you’re wondering if Murphy loves you.”

“Shit, I’m sorry. I really shouldn’t be acting like this,” Tate said. Rose was one of the few women Tate respected. She couldn’t believe she was being such a bitch to her.

“It’s about time you realized what a bitch you’re being. There’s a time and a place to get the claws out, honey. Now is not that time.

“What do you want me to do?” Tate asked, hating how right the other woman was being.

“Come to lockdown. Bring your new friend, and make it right with Angel. While you’re there, think about everything Murphy’s risking just to be with you.”

They finished off their lunch without another word.

MURPHY

Chapter Nine

Murphy sat at the bar in the club waiting for Rose to return. Hardy had sent him a text letting him know Tate and Rose were in the Italian place talking. Tiny had been beside himself with worry since he couldn't get Tate into the club for lockdown. Mikey handed him a beer, but he shook his head. "I'm waiting to see if Tate calls to be collected."

Killer sat beside him. "Do you think we should bring her friend?"

"I don't know. If she calls you can follow to bring Kelsey back with you," Murphy said.

"I can't ever recall Tate being like this. She was always so sensible, like her mother. Patricia knew lockdown was not something to joke about. Her mother would be embarrassed by her girl," Mikey said.

The older man looked scared. It was strange to see considering how much Mikey had lived through. The guy had more battle scars than he and Killer combined.

"Tate means a lot to all of us." Murphy reached out, putting a hand on Mikey's.

"Stop turning me into a pussy." Mikey pulled away, cursing.

"Right, that was Hardy," Tiny said, getting all of their attention. "Tate's being collected this afternoon from her apartment. Rose finally talked some sense into her."

Several cheers went around the room. Murphy wanted to laugh and smile. Instead, he sat and waited for the news.

"Three Lions have been spotted walking through town. They've been wearing their cut. The two cops that got killed, their families have been compensated and will be added to the roster for protection. They're coming in whether they like it or not. Butch and Zero took the van to bring them in. It's going to be crowded, but it's needed until we get a lid on everything. The Sheriff is making sure the folks know. Fort Wills is on guard."

The buzz from the news went around the room. "Do you know any of them?" Murphy asked, talking to Killer.

"No, Whizz and Time are working together some names. They'll have them to Tiny by tomorrow."

Tiny and Lash headed toward him.

"You're getting my daughter and bringing her here," Tiny said, poking a finger in his chest.

Murphy nodded. In the next instant, Tiny had his face pressed against the bar. He'd been expecting some kind of hurt from Tate's father and was surprised it had taken this long.

"I don't know what's going on between you and my daughter, but I'm going to find out. I know a lot of shit, Murphy. I like you, and I love my daughter. I'm keeping my shit together 'cause we've got other *shit* to handle." The pressure increased on his face. "I'm telling you that when this is over, you and me are going to have to resolve some issues," Tiny said. "Are you hearing me?"

"I'm hearing you," Murphy said.

"Good. Get your ass out of here and get Tate."

Murphy sat up, brushed his jacket down and cleaned any mess from his hair. No one was staring at him or Tiny. They must have been as prepared for the shit as he was. He was fucking the leader's daughter, and no one got away with that.

Heading out of the club, he grabbed his bike.

"Is she worth that?" Killer asked.

"What?" Murphy turned to the other man who he'd started to see as a friend.

"Tate, the daughter, is she worth the trouble you'll be in?"

"Hell, yeah, she's worth it. She's worth every single beating I'm going to get when she finally gives in." Murphy smiled, thinking about it.

"Why are you smiling?" Killer asked.

"Because when I've been beat down, I know Tate's going to be mine at the end of it." Straddling his bike, Murphy turned the key in the ignition. "You keep up?"

"Yeah."

Gunning his machine, Murphy headed to her apartment. Parking outside, he went straight through the front doors. Killer was seconds behind him. He didn't order the other man to get Kelsey. The only person Murphy wanted was Tate. Going up the three flights of stairs, Murphy knocked on her door waiting for an answer. He grabbed his piece from the back of his jeans and checked to see that it was loaded. A bad feeling was settling in the pit of his stomach. Something bad was going to go down. Tate opened the door. She held a single case in her hand.

"Let's go," he said.

"Hold on, what about Kelsey?" Tate asked.

"She's being taken care of."

"No, she has to come with us."

Holding her face between his hands, Murphy stared into her eyes. "She's being taken care of. Killer is getting her now."

Taking her hand he led her down the steps toward Kelsey's front door. Knocking once, he wasn't surprised to see Killer packing.

"You getting a bad feeling?" Murphy asked.

"Yeah. Something's not right. It could be me, but I don't know." Killer nodded at Tate before returning his gaze back to Murphy. "They're too desperate, and I think The Lions are going to do something stupid."

"I'm heading out. Be careful, and I'll see you at the compound." Murphy shook the guys hand and headed out. He kept Tate by his side, looking all around him. There was a tingling at the back of his neck. He glanced around, but nothing stood out to him. It was a quiet apartment block.

"What's going on, Murphy?" she asked.

"Keep down."

Something glinted off his mirror followed by the shattering of a window off his right shoulder. Falling to the ground he crushed Tate underneath him. Grabbing his cell phone and gun, he dialed the club's number.

Tate screamed. Her hands covered her head. "Murphy!"

"We've got to get cover," he said as more bullets rained down. Fuck, they were all over the place. Whoever was shooting were shit shots.

Glancing up he saw Killer covering Kelsey in the main building. No one had seen him yet as otherwise the doors would have been shot out.

Silence fell over the square, and he used the opportunity to move Tate. Grabbing her arm, he hauled her up and ran toward the back of the building. There was a wall overlooking the garden. Pushing her down, Murphy growled as something hit the side of his leg.

"What's going on? Someone is shooting at us? No one shoots at us." Tate was losing control. Her voice was high and grating on his nerves.

He slammed his lips down on hers trying to silence her. "Right now, baby, I need you to be quiet."

Glancing down at the burning pain in his leg, Murphy saw a bullet had grazed his outer leg. Fuck, that was going to sting when the adrenaline wore off.

He moved to glance behind the wall. Two men were arguing in the middle of the street carrying guns. Neither of them were wearing a cut. They looked insane to be arguing in front of him. Seeing the decoy, Murphy glanced behind them. There was a van with a window partially open. Squinting, he saw the guns pointing out. Whoever was firing the guns were not desperate men. Could it be The Lions? Fuck, he couldn't concentrate. His woman was with him, and he needed to get her to safety.

Fuck, his leg was stinging.

Putting the cell to his ear he waited for the guys to pick up.

"Hello, The Skulls place," Angel said.

Fuck, his fucking luck. A lot of fucks were needed.

Fuck. Fuck. Fuck. Fuck. Fuck!

"Angel, get Lash or any one of the guys."

"Murphy, how's Tate? I heard she's coming in?" Angel asked.

Fuck. She was too nice to get angry with.

"She's good."

Angel started talking, and Murphy was losing patience. Another round of firing, followed by shouting happened.

"Fuck, Angel, shut the fuck up. I've got bullets coming, and I'm open. Get one of the fucking guys now."

The woman screamed over the line. Hysterics erupted around them. Murphy tried to deal with it. Tate was crying; shouting was going, and then the sound of bikes in the distance interrupted him. Bullets sounded, and he looked over the wall in time to see Time and

Whizz pulling up. Time fired at the van, running at it while Whizz took the two decoys on

Turning to Tate, he calmed her down. “I need you to stay here. Don’t move until I get you.”

Kissing her lips, Murphy left her side, ignoring the pain in his leg.

Whizz had both men restrained, and the van was open.

“I couldn’t save the men,” Time said. “I don’t recognize them. They’re not Lions.”

Killer and Kelsey left the building. Murphy collected Tate from where he’d put her.

“I don’t know the club’s number, so I called my guys,” Killer said.

Looking at the mess in the van, Murphy shook his head. “This was a real hit. Something is going down.”

“Lions go after family. I thought The Skulls didn’t include family into the bargain,” Killer said.

Tate wrapped her arms around his waist. Murphy held her close. His heart was racing. Whoever had come to kill her had meant business. Tate was not supposed to survive this day.

“Something bad is going down,” Murphy said.

“Talk to me.” Her voice was small.

“Baby, you shouldn’t even be here.” There were two dead men on the floor and a third hanging out of the truck. Covering her eyes, Murphy left the van waiting for his club to arrive. Ten minutes later, the van was charging down the street. Hardy, Lash, Nash, and Tiny were clearly visible.

The moment the van was parked Tiny was out of the door. He ran toward Tate pulling her in close. Murphy watched the scene.

"Honey, you're okay? You're all right? Nothing happened. You've not been shot?" Tiny cupped her face, turning her head this way and that.

"Dad, I'm fine. If anything Murphy hurt me when he pushed me to the floor. I'm fine. Nothing happened."

Tiny stared into her face, shaking his head. "Nothing can happen to you. Do you fucking hear me?"

"I hear you, Dad." She was crushed in a hug, and Murphy smiled.

"Get in the fucking truck and take your friend with you. You're back at the compound. Eva's already there."

Tiny shoved her in the direction of the truck. Murphy squared his shoulders waiting.

"If anything had happened to my daughter I'd kill you slowly and make you wish you were dead long before I'd grant it."

"Understood."

"Thank you for getting her to safety." Tiny shook his hand then turned toward the van. "What we got?"

"I don't fucking know," Murphy said, filling him in on all the details.

"Leave one of the bikes here. Round this shit up and bring it back. I want to know what's going on."

"What are you going to do?" Killer asked, joining them.

"I'm going to find the threat to my daughter, and then I'm going to annihilate them," Tiny said.

"What if this has nothing to do with Tate? With The Skulls, the club comes first," Whizz said.

"Then some people are about to learn a very valuable lesson. No one fucks with my family. Tate, the club, it's all the same. It's all family, and family will always come first."

****

"He protected me, Tate. I never thought a guy was like that out there, but he is," Kelsey said.

Tate smiled at her friend as she relived the moments of the shooting. Kelsey looked in love. It was sweet but also dangerous. Tate didn't know Killer very well, but his name alone scared her. They were travelling back to the compound. She heard some of the men sniggering. Rolling her eyes, she kept her back to them.

"I'm sure he's a nice guy. I don't know anything about him, and I'd suggest you be careful around him," Tate said.

"I will. I promise." Kelsey grabbed her hand, squeezing it tight.

Back at the compound she saw Zero, Butch, Mikey, and Rose waiting. They all embraced her as she came out of the van. Seconds later, Killer, Whizz, and Time made it through followed by the van being driven by Hardy.

Kelsey was drawn into the embrace as well. Tate made the introductions, and they were rushed inside.

They showed Kelsey to a spare bedroom, and Tate took her old room. Walking past her friend's bedroom she saw Kelsey sat on the bed, white as a ghost.

"Are you all right?" Tate asked.

"It's suddenly dawning on me, we got shot at."

Tucking some hair behind her ear, Tate walked into the room, shutting the door behind her.

"Club life takes some getting used to," Tate said, taking a seat beside her.

"Did you get used to it? Has this happened often to you?"

"Several months back a rival gang broke into my dad's house and pointed a gun at me. I saw two prospects get shot and almost die. Eva, my nanny was shot, and Angel was as well. It was one of the first shootings I've seen. The Skulls don't usually include families, and we're left out of the equation."

"This time is different?"

"Yeah, I guess so."

Tate took Kelsey's hand like the other woman had done in the back of the van.

"We could have died today," Kelsey said.

"We didn't. We're here to tell the tale and drink and party." Tate looked down at her lap. "I'll understand if you don't want to be friends with me anymore. This takes a lot to digest, and you're not part of the life."

"I want to be your friend. I'm going to lie down and process everything that's happened, okay?"

"Yeah, I'll come and check on you soon." Tate squeezed Kelsey's hand and left the room silently. Killer was stood outside the door.

Tate stopped and looked at the other man.

"How's she doing?" he asked.

"Pretty shook up. It's to be expected. Being shot at is not something she's used to." Tate stared at him trying to get a good read of the man who clearly had a thing for her friend.

"What? You got a question, just ask."

"I don't know you. I've known most of these men my whole life, but I don't know you. I know you're from The Lions, and they were first class assholes. I didn't like them." She took a step closer and pressed a finger against his chest. "I've not known Kelsey very long, but I like her. She's a good woman. A great person. If you hurt her because of whatever shit you think women deserve then I'll hurt you. I'll castrate you and make you wish you'd never crossed me."

"You're a woman. You can't do anything to me."

Smiling, Tate reached down, grabbed his balls and twisted them. It was a move Murphy had showed her and one she remembered. Killer growled, covering her hand with his. She tugged and moved in close to whisper against his ear.

"I'm a woman. I've got a delicate nature. I've got tits, cunt, and an ass. I'm like a lot of women in a lot of ways, but I'm different." Looking into his eyes, Tate squeezed. "I'm my father's daughter, and I don't say shit I don't mean." She let him go and watched him fall to the floor. "Be warned, I will hurt you if you hurt my friend. You want to fuck around with people, use the sweet-butts. They don't expect anything better. Kelsey expects better, and she likes you. Make sure you give me a reason to like you."

She walked away without a backwards glance. Tate hoped her message got across to him. If not, the guy was in for some hard lessons.

Kelsey was only involved in The Skulls because of her. Tate would do everything in her power to protect her new friend. She found Angel working behind the bar with Mikey, one of the original members. Mikey left the bar and pulled her in for a tight hug.

"It's not been the same without you, honey," he said.

Hugging him back, Tate looked at Angel. The other woman had tears in her eyes.

"You keep getting shot at, and I'm going to have a heart attack." He kissed the top of her head.

"I'm not going to get shot. Murphy was there, and he saved me."

"I don't like those other boys he's with. They're not good."

"Mikey, you always put the guys through their paces. Everyone knows you hate change."

"Exactly, so when are you moving back home?" he asked.

"I'm not moving back home."

"Mikey, over here we need you," Tiny said, shouting across the room.

Rolling her eyes, Tate moved away going to Angel, giving Mikey some room. Sitting at the counter, she waited for the younger woman to speak.

"I've missed you," Angel said.

"I've missed you, too."

What more was she supposed to say? She felt like a total bitch for leaving the other woman behind.

Angel thrust a hand under Tate's eyes. "Look, I got married."

Taking hold of Angel's hand, Tate admired the ring. "I heard. Congratulations."

"I'm not going to take it personally. I get that you want some space away from this place, but, Tate, this is your family. They all care about you and worry. Tiny was freaking out with the phone call. I was freaking out. It's not good."

Lash entered going straight for Tate. "My girl was worried. You shouldn't be this hard to deal with, Tate."

"I know. I'm a bitch. I'm sorry." She glanced down at the counter, feeling the bile rise in her mouth. "Angel, you deserve better from me." Looking up, Tate focused on the woman she considered her friend. "I made a lot of mistakes the last couple of weeks. I've cut you off, and I shouldn't have done. Will you forgive me? And I promise I'll do better." She looked at Angel, hopeful.

"We're friends, Tate. I love you and miss you. I'd love for us to hang out again."

She let out a breath. "Thank you." Angel's forgiveness meant so much to her.

"Good. Murphy's asking for you," Lash said, kissing the side of Angel's neck. Dismissed, Tate walked around checking all the rooms. She found him sat in the laundry room. His pants were wrapped around his ankles, and he was cupping his junk.

"Fuck, be careful," he said, hissing.

"Stop being a fucking baby." A woman was knelt in front of him.

Tate cleared her throat.

"Tate, tell her she's being mean, and I did get shot." He lifted a hand toward her. She went to his side and gasped when she saw the graze on his thigh.

"It's not a shot. It's a fucking graze, and you're being a baby." The blonde looked at her, nodded, smiled and went back to work.

"Did you settle in okay?" Murphy asked, wincing. "Watch it."

The blonde kept working.

"I don't know you," Tate said.

The other woman looked up. "I'm Sandy."

"How come you're fixing him up?"

"I'm the current doctor in the house. I've got a week off, and I'm spending my time here."

Tate nodded. "Is Sandy your club name?"

"No, I get some shit from the guys at work, and I'm a real doctor."

"What are you doing here then?" Tate asked, surprised to see a doctor in the compound. Sandy was also very pretty, beautiful even. She clearly wasn't desperate for attention.

"It's easy sex. None of the guys want a commitment, and I'm more than happy being a doctor. I'm not looking for anything long term," Sandy said.

"Cool." Tate nudged his shoulder. "You're being used."

His eyes darkened. "Not me. The other guys."

"I've not fucked Murphy. Zero, Butch, and Mikey are the men I've fucked."

Tate laughed. “I’m sure you’re popular.”

“It’s fun.” Sandy slapped Murphy’s thigh. “I’ll check on it tomorrow, but otherwise you’re all good. There’s nothing to worry about. I’ve gave you a shot in case of infection. Keep it clean, and you’ll be fine.” She’d also covered it with a large bandage.

Sandy left the room leaving her alone with Murphy.

“I wanted to say thank you,” Tate said.

“Why?” He groaned as he lifted his jeans.

“You’ve been shot worse than this, and you’re complaining about a graze?” she asked, getting frustrated with all of his noises.

“It stings like a bitch. Stop being hard on my ass, and come here.” He wrapped an arm around her waist, pulling her toward him. His jeans were still open, but they rested around his waist.

“Dad could see,” she said, warning him.

“I don’t care. You’re mine, baby. Now kiss me.”

Smiling, Tate leaned in close brushing her lips against his. “Thank you,” she said, whispering against his lips.

“I’ll always take care of you.” He rubbed her nose with his.

Giggling, Tate pulled out of his arms and turned. Tiny stood in the doorway staring at them. The giggling died along with the smiling.

“You’re needed in the warehouse,” Tiny said.

Murphy cleared his throat and began buttoning up his jeans.

“Sandy cleaned him up. He should be good to go.”

“Good.” Tiny’s arms were folded as he gazed at her.

“What?” she asked.

"It's good to have you home. Haven't you got a hug for your old man?"

Stepping close, she wrapped her arms around his back. "Stop being a pain in the ass."

"Leave the room," Tiny said, speaking to Murphy.

She watched him disappear. Tiny closed the door.

"Dad, what are you doing?" she asked.

"In the last year you've been shot at twice. First in my house and now outside your apartment building." He cupped her cheeks between both of his palms. "It's two times too many."

"You can't be there for me all the time."

"I know. Steven and Blaine are going to be patched in when all this shit is through. The guys want them in. Any guy who takes a bullet for the women is good enough for me. They're staying here while we sort this shit out." Tiny's held her face tighter. "Be safe."

"I'll be safe, Dad, I promise."

"Eva's in my room. Talk to her, please. I don't want to lose her."

He started to leave, opening the door, ready to disappear.

"You've got to make a choice about her, Dad."

"What do you mean?" he asked, looking at her over his shoulder.

"She deserves a life. A life where a man loves her and takes care of her. She's been waiting for you for too long, and you're fucking sweet-butts when you can have her. Mom's dead, and she's not coming back. Please, for me, don't fuck this up."

He didn't say a word. She glanced down at the floor, feeling uncomfortable.

"I'll sort it out," he said, leaving her alone.

Letting out a breath, Tate wondered how her life had gotten so complicated. She was sorting out Kelsey and Eva's love lives.

Chapter Ten

Murphy sat in the back of the van glaring at the two men they'd taken from the street outside of Tate's apartment. They'd pissed themselves and vomited. The smell was making him feel sick. Killer, Zero, and Nash were sat in the back with Tiny and Mikey in the front. The rest of the men were at the compound protecting the families and friends.

"You're going to fucking die," Zero said.

One of the men whimpered. They were both shaking and sweating. Turning away from the scene, Murphy looked at Tiny. The other man hadn't looked at him.

Running fingers through his hair, Murphy knew he needed a haircut. Why the fuck was he thinking about his hair when they were about to torture these two men?

At the warehouse, three more of The Skulls were waiting. Stink, Gunn, and Pretty were waiting. Climbing out of the van, he shook the other guys' hands and pulled them in for a hug. He slapped them on the back, moving to the final guy.

"It fucking stinks in the back," Zero said. "You wouldn't know, Stink, because it smells like you."

Stink stuck his middle finger at Zero. It was known that Stink was called that because the guy couldn't smell anything. The guy had no sense of smell and could do a lot of the worst kind of jobs. Rumor was during his prospect days, Stink would whistle while being forced to clean the toilets at the compound. Nothing bothered the guy smell-wise.

Either way, Stink was a good man.

"Fuck you, Zero, you going faster than two strokes?" Stink asked.

Moving away from the group, Murphy wasn't ready to get into name calling. The guys could last a long time. Tiny walked with him. The others were getting the guys from the back of the van.

Grabbing the chairs, Murphy set everything up ready to watch.

"I think Killer can handle this, don't you? I want to see what he's about," Tiny said.

"Killer will be happy to hurt these guys for you. Providing it's not sport, he'll do anything you want." Murphy secured the chains to the hooks in the walls.

"Sport?" Tiny asked.

"The Lions used him to kill anyone. Some of the guys or women didn't even have to have a problem with the club. They just liked the control they had over Killer. He's a loyal son of a bitch and does everything he can for the club." Murphy shrugged. "He, Whizz, and Time were the only ones who didn't want to hurt Tate or go to their house. They were good guys for doing that."

They were silent as they worked. When the sound of commotion, laughing, and whooping came through the door, Tiny grabbed the cut of his leathers. "I've got an issue with you. You've been fucking my daughter, and you're going to pay the consequences for it," Tiny said.

"Fine. I love Tate, and I'll handle whatever shit you've got to throw at me."

Tiny let him go as the door opened. The whole club would know what's going on in no time at all. He'd pay the price for loving the leader's daughter, but until then, they had to deal with the threat on the club.

Both men were chained to the chairs that were in turn chained to the floor. They were screaming, shouting for help.

"Keep yelling. We're not going to leave here for some time. No one can hear you," Tiny said. "Killer?"

The other man looked up. "Get me the information that I need."

Killer walked toward the man. Murphy sat down on the sofa, waiting. He wasn't bothered by the sound of flesh hitting flesh, or the screams. Burning caused him a problem, and he left the warehouse for a smoke.

Nash followed him out to take a smoke.

"I can take all kinds of shit. It's part of the job, but I can't handle burning. They're talking and giving everything away," Nash said.

Murphy nodded. "We'll be given the heads up before we leave."

"Tiny's going to fuck you over with Tate. Is she worth it?"

Turning to Nash, he was surprised by the question. "You grew up with her."

"So? A bitch is still a bitch. Some women are not worth the problems."

"What about your brother? Did you think Angel was worth it?" Murphy asked.

"She's worth it. Angel makes my brother happy. Tate's pissed off with you over The Lion business."

"Yeah, she's pissed at me, but I'm not going anywhere. I love her, and I'm going to do everything I can to prove to her I'm not going anywhere." None of them got it. All they saw was the bitch. Turning to Nash, he stared at the other man. "You know, I fell in love with Tate when she was sweet and charming. I couldn't imagine my life being with anyone else. Time and what has happened between us has changed us both." Pulling on his cigarette, Murphy decided to open up to the other man. "There was a time I'd have been satisfied with Tate as she was back then, but now I know I'd have grown bored with her. Sure, I loved the way she was, and I still do. This club is my life, and the woman she was wouldn't be able to handle my shit. This bitchy woman, the brat, can handle everything I throw at her."

Smiling, he kept his gaze on Nash. "You all see her as a problem. To me, she's fucking perfect. I love her attitude. I relish the challenge she gives me, and I know deep down that she loves me, too. Tate is hard, and she's what I need. So, yeah, she can be a bitch and fight me and cuss, but I fucking love it 'cause I love her."

"Wow, you're really pussy-whipped," Nash said.

"Tate's worth it. I love everything about her."

"We're done, guys," Zero said, popping his head out of the door.

Flicking his smoke away, Murphy headed back inside.

"What's going on?" Nash asked.

"These fuckers were hired by drug dealers and pimps," Tiny said, kicking the leg of the nearest guy. Both men were lying on the floor, dead.

"They were terrified," Killer said, wiping his hands on a cloth.

"This shit has nothing to do with The Lions?" Murphy asked.

"No."

"What the fuck are drug dealers doing in Fort Wills? They're supposed to be the fuck out of the town. It's what we promised the fucking town," Nash said, cursing.

"I'm talking to the Sheriff and to Alex. He'll put the word out to see who's playing their cards close to our home," Tiny said.

"Close to home? They're not close to home, they're in fucking home," Mikey said.

The two older men glared at each other.

"We'll handle this," Tiny said.

"Yeah, we fucking will. No more running drugs, that's the way we deal with this. If Alex doesn't like it tell him to go fuck himself," Mikey said. "Your guilt over Patricia has nothing to do with this."

Tiny stepped closer to Mikey.

Murphy watched the room go tense.

"I'm not fucking guilty. Cancer took my woman, not the club. I deal with Alex for business," he said.

"Drugs are bad for business."

Murphy frowned. The Skulls had been transporting drugs out and away from Fort Wills for a long time. Why would now suddenly be different?

"What if they're connected?" Murphy asked.

"What?" Mikey and Tiny turned to him.

"The Lions were stupid. I mean, they were fucking stupid. I was with them for a couple of years, and none of them had the kind of cash or resources to the do the shit they did." Looking at Killer he tried to draw him into a conversation. "Drugs were always available for everyone, remember?"

"Yeah, Jeff would leave for days at a time, and when he got back, coke, money, and whores were always with him," Killer said.

"Maybe the shit that went down at your house those months ago wasn't The Lions like we thought, like I thought, but was Jeff acting out in desperation."

"Jeff was a crack head," Killer said. "He was hooked on drugs, but he was always fine apart from his rages."

The guys followed the leader they understood. The Lions admired Jeff for his ability to take charge. They were nothing like The Skulls. There were no morals in the other club.

"You think the druggies were bank rolling, or do you think they came to collect a debt and Jeff didn't have the money?" Tiny asked.

"It could be one or the other," Murphy said. "Think about it. Druggies want in Fort Wills. They owned this town once before, so what better way than to get a rival club to take out The Skulls? That's theory one. The second theory is Jeff was a crack head, and he owed lots of money. The Skulls have money, and he needed it. Both theories work."

"It's too close to home," Tiny said, tossing a table over. "My daughter almost got killed in my own fucking town!"

Murphy and the rest of the men watched as Tiny finally lost it. The other man had been keeping his shit together for far too long.

"Should we stop him?" Killer asked.

"No, he needs to do this."

Tiny lifted up the comfortable chair in the centre of the room. All the guys winced as Tiny launched it against the wall breaking it. All of them had to sit or sleep in that chair while working at the warehouse. Tiny had just destroyed one of the few pieces of furniture that was comfortable.

"He's so replacing that," Zero said.

"Fucking pussy," Stink said.

"Shut up," Mikey said, slapping both men around the back of the head.

Murphy smirked but didn't say a word.

****

Tate sat with Eva, Angel, Rose, and Kelsey at one of the tables. Several of the men were muttering about babysitting duty. Blaine was sat beside them with his woman, Emma, and little girl, Darcy.

Angel and Blaine were great friends in the most unusual kind of way. Tate had watched them getting close. There weren't any intimate feelings between the two. Angel was the one responsible for Blaine getting his woman and kid back.

She glanced at Eva to see her downing another shot.

"Are you all right?" Tate asked.

"I'm fine. I'm just going to get drunk, and then Tiny can know what it's like cleaning drunken people up." The shot was replaced with another. Rose chuckled.

"It's how our men learn. Hardy would come home stinking of perfume because of the sluts rubbing against him. I went out the next night, rubbing against men. When I came home, there was yelling along with the best fuck I've ever had," Rose said.

"There won't be any sex, no, that's a mistake to have sex," Eva said. "Does he think it was good? I mean, Tiny's the leader of this fucking club, and he's got sluts fucking him all the time, but they don't get to talk about his technique." Eva stopped to take another shot. Angel and Kelsey were giggling, sipping from their own beer. "I mean, he's got the equipment, but I didn't come once. He humped, groaned, and that was it."

Eva then imitated some sounds that just disturbed Tate.

"Guys, are you forgetting this man's my father? Ew," Tate said, covering her ears.

"Not to mention my boss," Blaine said, looking sick. "You women are tough cookies."

"We're the *old ladies* of the men," Rose said, shouting the words. "We've got a lot of shit to put up with."

The sweet-butts were sat together. Some were a bright red, but none of them said anything. Tate refused to feel bad for them. They all chose to be the women who fucked the men.

Sandy took a seat. Tate waited for Rose to send her away.

"I'm not just any sweet-butt," Sandy said. "I fuck the men who are not taken. I told you, easy sex, nothing else. I don't want to be an old lady."

"She doesn't. Zero offered her the chance to be his wife," Rose said. "She turned him down flat."

Eva took another shot, and Tate shook her head.

"So, is Murphy good in the sack?" Sandy asked.

"Excuse me?" Tate looked up at the blonde haired woman. The men stopped to look at her.

"It's no secret. Tiny already knows about it." Sandy poured herself a drink. "I just wanted to know seeing as you've had to listen to prowess about your father."

Laughing, Tate shook her head. "I wish he wasn't a good fuck, but he is. I hate him so much."

The table burst into fits of laughter. Tired of not drinking, she downed three shots in a row and then lined up another three. She needed the buzz from the alcohol to get her through the rest of the night.

Emily left with Darcy, and the rest of the children were put to bed. With Eva and Rose's help Tate got the rest of the girls drinking. Angel and Kelsey were now swaying from side to side. The empty tequila bottle was changed for a full one. Wandering over to the sound system, Tate put on a song and started dancing.

Steven caught hold of her shoulders. "You need to stop this."

"It's lockdown. I'm bored, drunk, and want to dance. Back off," she said.

Rose was up on the table, and Hardy crashed through the front doors. He'd left to take a look around the perimeter.

"Baby, what the fuck are you doing?" Hardy asked.

"Dancing. Go and do your job. I'm having some fun with the girls." Rose pulled Eva onto the table.

Tate giggled as Eva threw the nanny gown from her shoulders and became the sensual woman she'd always known Eva was. Angel grabbed Kelsey while Sandy grabbed Blaine. Tate chuckled. Seeing the uncomfortable look on his face, she decided to go and save him. Replacing him with herself, Tate danced with the blonde. Sandy had some moves. They rubbed together, and Tate was shocked when the other woman slammed her lips down on hers.

The kiss wasn't awful, and it shocked her into silence.

Sandy pulled away, kissing down to her ear. "Did I also mention I was bi, and I'm seriously wet for you? You're fucking hot, Tate."

Her mouth fell open, and words completely failed her. What the fuck was she supposed to say?

"Erm, I'm flattered."

Sandy gripped her ass, tugging her close. "You should be more than flattered. If Murphy isn't blowing your world, give me a call. I'm more than happy to show you what a real woman feels like."

"What the fuck is going on here?" Tiny's voice cut across the music. The room fell quiet as the music was shut off.

Glancing over Tate saw Murphy watching her.

Smiling, she stroked Sandy's cheek and kissed the other woman's lips.

"Look, it's the leader. Quick, he's going to rock your world, not!" Eva said, laughing. Rose didn't help matters by encouraging the other woman.

Tate watched them climb off the tables. Angel was the first to launch herself into Lash's arms, since he had entered the club with the men.

"Baby," Angel said. "I'm horny."

"And drunk," Lash said, glaring at Tate.

She gave him a wave in kind.

They disappeared.

Kelsey ran for the bathroom, no doubt about to throw up. She saw Killer follow after her.

Hardy held Rose back as Eva made her way toward Tiny.

"Guess what, buster? I'm drunk, and I can now say this to you."

Tate winced as Eva stumbled over her words.

"You are a bastard. You've broken my heart more times than I can count, and if what you've got to offer at Vegas is all then the sweet-butts can have you." She hiccupped. "You're terrible in bed." She slapped Tiny and walked away with her head in the air.

Covering her mouth, Tate tried to cover her laughter.

It was her turn, and she walked up to Murphy. "If we're going to do this then let's make it official." Wrapping her arms around his neck, Tate brought him down for a kiss. Smashing their lips together, she deepened the kiss by plunging her tongue into his mouth.

After several seconds, he caught her against him, kissing her back. Pulling away from him she turned to her father.

"You can't do a thing about it because you've got to handle Eva."

Grabbing Murphy's hand she headed toward her bedroom. The silence was deafening. She didn't care. Getting her man to a room and naked was her only priority.

"We'll deal with you tomorrow," Tiny said.

Waving a hand in the air, Tate kept going 'til she got to his bedroom. Opening the door, she slammed him up against the nearest wall.

"You're drunk," Murphy said.

"So, I just declared us a couple. A few drinks isn't going to change that." She shoved his leather jacket from his shoulders followed by his shirt.

"Your father's going to kick my ass."

"A few bruises will look hot. Fuck me, Murphy. Make it count." She tugged the shirt from her body, throwing it to the floor.

He took over, unbuckling his jeans and stepping out of them. His fingers sank into her hair, and he brought her in close for a kiss. "Give me those fucking lips," he said.

Tate puckered, sending him a kiss through the air.

"Tease." He caught her close, pressing his advantage and claiming her lips.

She moaned, feeling lightheaded as his free hand roamed her body.

"I love you, baby," he said.

Gasping, Tate jerked back looking at him.

"I've loved you for a long fucking time. I know I fucked up, and I promise I'll never fuck up again. I'll spend the rest of our lives making it up to you." Both hands held her face in his. "You just announced we're a couple to your father. This is how it's going to be between us. I'm going to get my ass kicked, and you're going to be there when it's over."

Covering his hands, Tate wished she could deny everything he said. The hurt he'd caused her had been immeasurable. But she couldn't deny her feelings for him now, which was way more important.

Can I live without him?

Staring into his eyes, she glanced down his body where he'd gotten her name inked into his skin. She was with him forever.

Capturing his face in the same hold that he held her, Tate looked at him. "No more women or missions or shit. This is between us, and it's real."

"Yes to everything."

Licking her lips she nodded her head. "I love you, too."

He changed their positions pushing her up against the wall. His lips were everywhere, her mouth, her nose and down her neck. The possession of his hands and lips consumed her.

Pushing him away, she smiled. "Don't start thinking you can get away with shit."

"I don't expect to." He took her lips as he worked her pants down her thighs. "I expect you to be a hard assed bitch to me when I deserve it."

Chuckling, Tate circled his neck, bringing him close.

"Now, shut up so I can fuck you."

He walked her toward the bed. She shook her head.

"I don't think so." Turning him, she pushed him to the bed and followed him down. "I'm going to be in charge." She straddled his waist, biting down on his lip.

"So fucking good," he said, gasping.

She smiled, nibbling on his neck. "We're going to have some fun. Tomorrow you're going to get your assed kicked and will be all bruised. I won't be able to do what

I want." She sucked on his neck. "Let's have plenty of fun tonight."

He threw her to the bed, and she watched him reach for the drawer beside her bed. Murphy held a pair of police cuffs in his finger.

"Where did you get them?" she asked. Her pussy pulsed with a fresh wave of arousal.

"A guy owed me a favor. What do you say, Tate? Are you in the mood for a bit of kinky fun?"

Staring at the cuffs and then at him, Tate smiled. "Baby, I'm ready for anything."

Chapter Eleven

Wrapping the cuffs around a pole in the head board, Murphy locked her hands in place. His cock was so tight, and he was so horny he felt like he was going to come in his pants.

"Be prepared for your turn," she said, panting.

Dropping his hand between her thighs, he stroked through her wet slit feeling her hot tight heat.

"You're so wet for me. I'm going to have some of my fun first." Plunging two fingers into her cunt, he pumped them in deep. With his thumb he pressed against her clit, feeling her pussy tighten around his digits inside her. "I'll take my turn. I get you all to myself and at my mercy."

Releasing her body, he licked the cream off his fingers. "I've got a few other surprises with you in mind."

Murphy left the bed to get his box of tricks.

"You can't leave me like this," she said, moaning.

"I'm not going anywhere." He fisted his cock to show her his own need. "I need you just as much as you need me."

She jerked her head, whimpering as he showed her the vibrator he'd bought for her. "I'm here to give you everything you need."

Turning the vibrator on, he pressed the buzzing machine against her clit.

Tate cried out, jerking on the cuffs. He placed a pillow under her hands giving her space to move without them hurting.

Replacing the vibrator back to her clit, he found the other dildo he'd purchased. Everything in the box was for Tate.

"This is not fair," she said, panting. "I wanted a nice quick fuck."

"Sorry, baby. You got me all to yourself."

Bending down, he licked a circle around her nipple, lavishing it with his saliva before sucking the tip into his mouth. Her back arched off the bed, following his mouth.

"Not fair." She cried out, and her legs shut around his hand.

"You can come anytime you want. If you think kissing a woman is not going to make me stake my claim on you again, you've got another think coming," he said, biting down hard on her nipple.

Pushing the vibrator into her pussy, Murphy watched as she rode the vibrator toward orgasm. Her cries faded away as she lay on his bed. Tracing her ink, Murphy waited for her to regain her senses.

She looked at him smiling.

"That's one to me," he said.

Moving to the bottom of the bed, Murphy opened her legs and crawled up them to settle down directly over her mound. "Now I want to feel you come with my lips on you."

He eased the lips of her sex open with his fingers seeing the jewel of her clit glinting up at him. The scent coming off her was driving him crazy, making his mouth water. He wanted to soak in her musky scent, knowing he was the cause for turning her on.

"So fucking sexy," he said.

With his tongue he swirled around the jewel never once sucking her into his mouth. Her taste was exquisite, the best thing he'd ever tasted.

Pressing three fingers into her core, Murphy worked her open, pounding her pussy with his hand as he sucked her clit into his mouth. She shuddered, moaned, screamed, cried out, and begged for him not to stop. He wouldn't let up. Her hands were bound above the bed stopping her from escaping him.

She was completely at his mercy, and he loved every second of it.

"Mine, mine, mine," he said, muttering the words against her pussy.

Tate tensed up, and he felt the second climax taking hold of her. Throughout it all, he rode the wave with her, biting down on her clit and pumping into her warm sweetness.

Glancing up he saw her staring down at him.

"I think two will do you now." He found the key, releasing her hands from the cuffs. In one quick move he put her to her knees and grabbed the lube from the same drawer he'd taken the cuffs.

Easing enough over his length, he coated his cock before applying plenty to her ass.

"You're going to fuck my ass," she said.

"Yes, you're going to love it. You've ridden the rubber cock, so you can take mine." Throwing the tube away from him, Murphy pressed the tip of his cock to her ass. "Breathe out." He told her what to do, waiting as she complied with his demands.

Tate didn't keep him waiting. She did as he instructed. He pushed the tip of his cock inside her, watching her ass open around his length.

"Do you feel the burn, baby?" he asked.

"Shut up and fuck me."

Slapping her ass, Murphy pushed forward sending another inch into her anus.

Tate cried out, slamming back against him. He held her hips steady, refusing to let her take the lead.

He spanked her ass a couple more times for good measure. "You're not the one in control here, Tate. I am."

"I'm burning up, Murphy. Please, I need you to do something to make this aching stop."

Reaching around her body, he found her clit and started to stroke her. "How's that? Is the burn easing?"

She nodded, moaning into the sheets.

With her distracted, Murphy slammed the last few inches into her ass. Tate's screams were muffled by the bed.

"That's it. My cock is in your ass, Tate."

He swirled a finger around her nub feeling her ass tighten around his cock.

"Please, move or do something. I can't wait anymore," she said.

Bringing her to orgasm first, Murphy wouldn't find his own pleasure until he knew Tate was having a good time. Taking her ass was about their mutual pleasure, not him just getting his rocks off in a kinky kind of way.

"Come for me, Tate. Let me hear you scream."

He pumped his hips gently, sensing her need for more. Murphy sensed how close she was to letting go. Gripping her hip, he worked his length out of her ass and then eased back inside. He took his thrusts slowly, working her ass to accept him.

"Tell me how it feels, baby," he said.

"I feel so full. It burns and aches, and I don't want it to stop. Everything is crashing together."

Her head landed on the pillow cutting off her words.

Teasing her clit, Murphy gave up on drawing everything out. Tate needed to find her release, and he was going to give it to her.

Sinking into her ass, he felt her climax seconds before her screams rent the air letting him know she was climaxing. Rubbing her clit, he rode her ass hard finding his own release inside her hidden depths. He growled, joining her into bliss.

His fingers tightened on the hip he was holding as he pumped everything of himself into her ass.

Collapsing down beside her, he remained in her ass and simply held her in his arms.

She was panting for breath, like him. Murphy stroked her stomach, needing to touch a part of her in order to keep himself grounded.

"You're making me addicted to your touch," she said, snuggling in close.

"Is it working?" He kissed her neck, holding her tightly.

"I never thought I'd love being fucked in the ass, but yeah, it's working."

Tate covered her hands with his. "Daddy's going to kick your ass tomorrow."

He chuckled. "You've only just realized the consequences for your actions?" Biting down on her shoulder, Murphy let out a sigh. "I wouldn't have it any other way. Even if you were drunk when you did it."

"I wasn't totally drunk. I just needed a little courage to get me to do it. After what Eva did, something needed to break the ice."

"Yeah, I think Eva's going to be paying for calling him crap in bed." Murphy breathed in her scent.

"Stalker," she said, slapping his hand.

"What?"

"You're breathing in my scent. It's creepy."

Laughing, Murphy didn't say a word. There were no words for how this woman made him feel. Tate meant everything to him, and he thought he'd lost her because of his actions. He wouldn't change what happened as he'd become a spy in order to protect her. Everything else he'd change. There would never have been women.

They'd pushed women at him and watched until he had no choice but to fuck them in front of the club. He'd hated every second of his time with The Lions.

She was the only person who got him through the dangerous times of his life. Pushing the hair off her face he looked down at her.

"I really do love you," he said, looking at her.

Her face softened. "I love you, too."

"Thank you for giving me another chance."

"You're growing soft," she said, kissing his lips.

"No, I'm not soft. I'll kill when I need to. You'll be the only one to see me soft."

Tate started to giggle as he tickled her body. She tried to push him away. Pulling out of her ass, Murphy picked her up in his arms. She squealed, holding onto him.

"Will you stop doing that?" she asked, clawing at his skin.

"We need to wash, and then we're going to come back and sleep."

****

Tate sat on Murphy's bed, brushing out the tangles in her hair. She wore one of his shirts, and he was walking around the room butt naked. Her heart raced as she looked at him, strutting his stuff. The shower they'd taken together hadn't been quick. Murphy started by washing her, and then he'd gone to his knees before her, lifted one leg onto the ledge and begun to lick her pussy.

"What are you looking for?" she asked, putting the brush down.

"Scissors. Hair's fucking irritating me."

Getting up from the bed, she walked into his bathroom and retrieved the scissors. "Bring a stool and come and sit." She laid a towel on the floor then waited for him to come through. He carried one of the stools that were in his bedroom. Pointing to the floor, she ordered him where to put it. Tapping the seat she waited for him to sit.

"You're going to play hairdresser?" Murphy asked.

"I'll do a better job of it than you. I know what I'm doing." She didn't have a clue what she was doing, but it would be better than him just grabbing fistfuls of hair and chopping it off.

"It's only hair. It always grows back."

Shaking her head, she picked some up and started to work the length off with the scissors. She'd put him in front of the mirror in the bathroom. He was staring at her intently.

"What happened at the warehouse today?" she asked.

"Club business and you don't need to know."

Dropping the scissors to the floor, Tate walked out of the bedroom.

Grabbing her clothes she headed toward the door.

"What the fuck are you doing?" he asked, charging for the door. He stood in front of it blocking her exit.

"I'm not going to be one of the sweet-butts you fuck and enjoy. I'm not made like Angel, Rose, and Eva. If I'm going to be part of your life then you need to bring me into your world. You're going to have to involve me in your world."

"It's not how The Skulls work."

"I know, but if you don't make changes for us, Murphy, there won't be an us." She folded her arms refusing to back down.

"Tate," he said.

"No, no Tate this or Tate that. It's pretty simple. You're going to come home bruised, bleeding, and probably covered in blood, and you're going to expect me to pretend I didn't see anything?" Tate stared at him waiting to see her words register to him. "I'm a lot of things, Murphy, but playing dumb is not something I can do. I won't interfere, and even my dad won't know what I know. I can do that for you."

"It's dangerous."

"I've had a gun pulled on me twice. I need to know what shit is going down, or I walk. That's my final offer," she said.

He stared at her. "This is not negotiable?"

"It's not."

"Fine, then I don't want any woman with her lips on yours."

"Make sure my lips aren't available for anyone else," she said, counteracting his argument.

"You're one tough bitch to please, do you know that?" Murphy asked, smiling.

"I'll be the only bitch you've got to please. You're not going to get it easy. I grew up with Tiny, remember that. I've got his genetics inside me."

"Don't I fucking know it." He took her hand, leading her back to the bathroom. She watched him go under the sink producing a pair of hairdressing shears. "These are for you to finish the job," he said.

He sat down, staring at her in the reflection of the bathroom mirror.

"The two guys who were shooting at you, we took them to the warehouse."

"Did they know anything?" she asked.

Murphy told her everything. She saw it in his eyes, the fear he held at what he was doing. Tate knew he hated sharing with her, but it meant so much to her. Also, she knew he wouldn't be able to handle lying to her. This was their only solution. No matter what he told her, she wouldn't judge him at all.

"You did what you had to do, Murphy. There's no shame in that," she said, looking at him in the mirror.

"You're not seeing me differently?" he asked.

Leaning forward she pressed her lips to his. "No, I don't. This is your life, and I'm sharing it with you. You can share what you want with me. There's no need for you to hide."

Murphy wrapped his hand around the back of her neck. "Thank you."

She watched him visibly relax as he started talking once again, opening up about his world. Tate could do this for him. He wasn't alone in the world, and she'd stand beside him no matter what he did as a Skull.

There's more to this than him putting the club first.

Tate didn't even resent the fact the club was coming first. She was slowly accepting how important the club was, not that she'd tell anyone yet.

She listened as he talked about Killer getting the information out of the other man. The Skulls never gave anything away to their women.

"Do you trust Killer, Time, and Whizz?" she asked when he'd finished talking about everything that happened. She didn't like the thought of a drug group in Fort Wills. Tiny would end it at the first opportunity.

"I know they're hard guys to trust because of The Lions, but I vouched for them."

"If they go wrong, Murphy, your ass is on the line for bringing them in."

"They won't," he said.

Turning on the electric shears, she finished off his hair, removing a lot of hair as she did. All the time he looked at her, talking.

"Do you think we're crazy for putting the drugs with The Lions?" he asked.

She smiled. "No, I don't think it's crazy. Putting them together is logical. You can't dismiss the two."

Tate finished cutting his hair. "All done."

He caught her hand, bringing her down close. "Thank you."

Watching him walk out of the bathroom, Tate quickly cleaned away the mess and took a long hard look at her reflection.

You can do this, Tate. You can do this.

She couldn't live like Angel, accepting Lash's life without knowing the details of what went on. Growing up with The Skulls, Tate knew a lot of shit went down that she wouldn't want to know.

Murphy.

Her love for that man was far greater than her fear of knowing the truth. Turning off the light she found him sitting on the bed staring at the floor.

"I never touched a woman until they ordered me to fuck one," he said.

Freezing by the door, Tate stared at him.

"I was in the club for a year. Jeff was high as a fucking kite. He didn't know what he was doing. He threw a woman at me. She was drugged, but she wanted it. I told him no, and he pulled a gun on me." Murphy turned to look at her. There was no emotion in his face. "When I took the mission for Tiny, I promised *myself* no other women. You're my woman. Only Tate. I had no choice. A gun was pointed at my head, and I fucked her."

Tears filled her eyes as she imagined Murphy in such a position.

"When it was over, he ordered me to fuck another and then another. Afterwards, I scrubbed myself raw. I drew blood, but it wasn't enough. I then went to a clinic and got tested. I got tested every month to make sure I was clean."

Moving away from the door, she took a seat next to him on the bed. Grabbing his hand, she held him tightly, trying to offer him comfort.

"You don't have to talk about it," she said.

"I do have to talk about it."

"Waiting for those results were the fucking worst moment of my life," he said.

"What would you have done if you'd gotten something you couldn't fix?" she asked. This was a whole other side to the past. She'd only ever thought about her feelings and what he'd done to hurt her. Never once had she considered what he was going through. Tate hated her selfishness.

Murphy chuckled. "I couldn't come back to you broken. I decided if I caught something that couldn't be fixed, I was going to get everything Tiny needed to put The Lions down for good, and then I was going to kill myself by taking a gun to my own head."

Tate gasped, finding it hard to breath. "You were going to kill yourself?" she asked, not really believing his words.

"When I tell you they were the worst years of my life, I'm not kidding, Tate. I hated every fucking day. Jeff killed some of his own members to show how powerful he was. Being on the other end of his gun was the worst thing ever. Being forced to fuck women that were not you killed me inside. All the time I thought about you. Every time I got the all clear it was another lifeline."

Sitting in his lap, Tate held him close. "It's fine. I've got you. I'm not going anywhere, and neither are you. We've got each other, and that's all we need." Closing her eyes, Tate allowed herself to feel the pain of losing him. No, she couldn't have handled him going.

Grabbing his face, she stared at him hard. "No matter what happens, Murphy, I will always love you. You'll never be broken to me." Tears were filling her eyes. "You can always come to me."

He kissed her hard.

Murphy eased back on the bed with her in his arms.

"I'm not letting you go. I fought too hard to have you already," he said.

"I'm here, Murphy, and I'll be here when you wake up. I'm not going anywhere. Whatever you need, I'm here for you." Her words were so true.

"There she is," he said. Frowning, she stared into his eyes. "You can be a bitch all you want and I need that, but I see the woman I fell in love with."

She'd not let anyone in for a long time. Murphy was seeing the real her, the woman she kept hidden from everyone else. Instead of pulling away, she kept staring at him, wanting to be open to him.

"You can't disappear anymore," he said.

"I don't want to, Murphy."

Settling down on top of him, Tate closed her eyes, holding him. He was warm, hard, and everything she wanted in a man.

Forgive him, and let the past go.

She already had.

Chapter Twelve

Murphy watched her sleeping, and seeing her peaceful sent joy running through him. Her hand rested across her name inked onto his abdomen. Running his fingers up and down her arm, he didn't want to leave her. It was morning, and the club was already awake and alive with activity. Sleeping in her arms was the best night he'd ever spent.

"You're so beautiful," he said.

There was a knock on the door. Lash stuck his head around the door. Murphy made sure Tate was covered. The other man had grown up with Tate, but he wasn't letting another man eyeball his woman.

"Tiny's waiting for you. Leave her here," Lash said.

Nodding his head, Murphy curled her around his pillow making sure he wouldn't wake her. This was what he had to do in order to make Tate his woman. Grabbing his clothes, Murphy dressed while watching her sleep. She looked so beautiful, and he'd gladly get his ass kicked in order to be with her.

Kissing the top of her head, Murphy left the room. He passed several of his brothers on the way down. Holding his head high, he saw they were all looking at him with respect. Lash was waiting for him outside the backdoor. There was an open space where the men could let off some steam and shoot some hoops.

"Isn't this a little dangerous?" Murphy asked.

"Perimeter has been checked. We've got some guys on the roof keeping a look out. Tiny doesn't want to wait. He had a bad night, and you've got an ass whopping to answer to," Lash said.

Looking back, he saw Angel twisting her hands together watching him. “If she wakes up keep her in here.”

Angel jerked her head in response.

Following Lash outside, he heard the door close. Tiny was stood in the middle of the yard. The older man wasn’t wearing a shirt, and Murphy saw the ink holding Tate’s and Patricia’s names.

“You should have known this was coming,” Tiny said.

“I knew, and I’m more than prepared to take what I deserve.” Pulling his cut from his shoulders, Murphy tugged his shirt from his shoulders. Tate’s name was clear to see across his abdomen.

Lash, Nash, Zero, and Killer were stood watching.

“You think you’re good enough for my daughter?” Tiny asked, circling his arms, getting ready for a fight.

“I’m the only person good enough for her, and you know it.” He went to stand a few feet away from him.

“No, you’re a piece of shit, Murphy. You didn’t even stay around and volunteered to get away at the first opportunity. Tate’s worth more than that.” Tiny stepped closer. He looked ready to kill.

Clicking his knuckles, Murphy stepped closer. “Everything I did was for Tate. They were all a danger to her and to her town. She has a right to walk around her town and feel safe.”

Tiny growled.

“You can fight me and I’m more than happy to take a beating, but I’m not going to walk away.”

He saw the first punch. Murphy took the hit that went square to his jaw.

“I love her,” Murphy said.

Another hit to his stomach.

Bending over, Murphy gasped for breath.

The other brothers watching the fight winced at the hit.

"You shouldn't say shit like that," Lash said.

"I love her, and I'm going to make her happy." Murphy blocked the next hit and shoved Tiny back. "Listen to me."

"No more talking." Tiny charged him.

Murphy found a weak spot, lashing out and cutting three hits to Tiny's ribs. The older man didn't back away but kept coming for more. Blocking a few more hits, Murphy didn't anticipate his legs being taken out from under him.

Landing on the floor with a thump, Murphy cried out as his whole bode was jolted. There was nothing for Tiny to grab onto. Kicking up, he pushed Tiny away giving him chance to get back to his feet.

"She's my daughter. You should never have touched her." Tiny yelled the words across the forecourt.

"I never wanted to love her. I did everything I could to stay away." Murphy held his hands out toward Tiny. "It was too hard to fight her. She's beautiful, smart, and tough as nails."

"I know. She's my daughter." Tiny lost his temper charging at him. "No man should touch her."

"Dad, stop it," Tate said, yelling across the yard. It was too late, and Murphy went down. He tried to block the hits, but they were coming too fast.

Glancing toward Tate he saw Lash holding her back.

"Get fucking off me."

"Tiny, get off that boy now!" Eva's voice cut through the fight. Tiny paused and looked in the direction of where the voice came from.

"Leave him alone." Tate ran toward him, going to her knees beside him. He wanted to be a man and tell her to back away. The sweet, tender look on her face was too hard to deny.

"Tate, back off," Tiny said.

"You've made your point. He's not to hurt me, and he'll answer to you. Murphy gets it, and you need to back away." Tate knelt beside him, protecting him.

He fell deeper in love with her for trying to protect him.

"He hurt you. I'm not going to let you throw your life away on this piece of scum." She got to her feet and shoved Tiny away.

"He hurt me once. You've been hurting Eva repeatedly. You don't deserve her. What are you going to do when her father comes to call? What if her father is a hard-nosed bastard just like you?" Tiny went to speak, but Tate held her hand up. "No, you've done enough. I don't need you to defend my honor. I love him, and you're not going to stand in the way of that."

Murphy got to his feet putting Tate behind him. "I will never hurt her again." Fuck, he ached all over. Tiny knew where to put his fists to make it count. Coughing, Murphy faced his leader. "I'll take every hit, and I'll do everything you need me to in order to win back your trust. I'm not going away."

Before Tiny could say anything else, Butch called to them. "Nash, there's a woman here asking for you."

"Tell her to fuck off. I've got more pressing drama to deal with," Nash said.

"She called you Edward and said her name was Sophia. Her face is badly bruised, and she's hysterical."

No one could stop him as Nash charged toward Butch. Murphy heard the commotion. Chaos ensued as Tiny's name was called.

"Dad, give him your blessing," Tate said.

Her father pointed his finger at Murphy's chest. "You hurt her and I'll fucking end you."

Tiny ran toward the club.

"He really hurt you," Tate said, pressing on his bruised sides.

"No, it was worth it. I've got you by my side." Murphy pulled her against him, holding her close. He ached all over, but he got his woman at the end.

Zero whistled, gaining their attention. "You two need to come inside."

Heading in, Murphy wrapped his arms around her shoulders.

The instant they stepped inside he heard the hysterical woman speaking. Nash was stood in front of a woman with midnight black hair and blue eyes. One side of her face was badly bruised and her lip bleeding.

"T-t-they said to c-c-come here. T-t-they took her, Edward."

"Who? Who did they take?" Nash asked.

"Kate. She's gone. She was on drugs, and they killed her." Sophia broke down. "My sister, they killed her."

This was Kate's sister, the woman Nash was in love with. She was nothing like how Murphy imagined her. Sophie was a full figured woman with large tits, small waist, and flared hips. She was the complete opposite of Kate. What the hell did Nash see in Kate?

Kate? Fuck, the sweet-butt was dead.

Nash wrapped his arms around her. "We'll figure this out. I promise, Soph, I won't let anything happen to you."

"Kate was on drugs?" Tiny asked.

"What's going on?" Tate asked, squeezing his arm.

"Nash has a thing for Kate's sister. I'm guessing that's the woman who he wants. She doesn't look very good."

He watched the other man wrap his arms around Sophia's shoulders as she slumped toward him.

"I didn't know she was using. I'd have gotten her off," Sophia said.

"What about you? You're the one with her at all times. Was she using?" Tiny turned toward Nash. If the other man knew Kate was using, the shit was going to hit the fan. Tiny didn't allow the drugs in the family or the club.

"No, I would have reported it immediately."

"She looks a little like Angel," Tate said, drawing his attention back to her.

Murphy chuckled.

A large boom rang out, and dust filled the club.

"Incoming!"

Another bang rang out shaking the foundations of the club. Tate screamed as gunfire rang out.

"Get down." Murphy pushed her to the floor, covering her head and body with his.

"What's happening?"

Murphy saw the others doing the same. Tiny was on top of Eva, Lash on Angel. The women were all protected.

"Weapons, get your pieces," Tiny said, yelling."

The main wall of the building crumbled as a truck rammed into the wall. "Fuck," Murphy said, pulling Tate out of the way. Men filled into the room. He didn't recognize any of them.

Trying to get his woman out of the way, Murphy turned to grab a weapon from the wall. It was all it took as screaming ceased.

"Shut the fuck up," a man said, yelling. A gun was fired up to the ceiling.

Turning around, Murphy froze. Someone he didn't recognize had hold of Tate with a knife against her throat. There were no leather cuts or discernible marks.

"Murphy," she said, squeezing the words out. The fear on her face would stay with him forever.

"So, you're the one I've been looking for," the man said, staring at him.

Looking around the chaos of the compound, Murphy saw they were all surrounded with men he didn't recognize at all.

"What do you want?" he asked, settling his piece behind his back.

Staring at Tate, he tried to think, to focus.

"Jeff told me a lot about you. He said you were loyal, and I've been watching you for some time."

"What's your name?" Glancing to his left he saw Tiny collapsed on the floor, blood pooling around him.

Fuck. Fuck. Fuck. Fuck.

He saw Killer, Time, and Whizz were moving around outside of the truck. The three men were not locked on by the shooters. What the fuck were they doing? Fuck, all The Skulls had a gun pointed at them, and someone he didn't know wanted to talk to him.

"Call me Sal."

The name rang a bell. "You're Jeff's supplier?" Murphy asked

"That's right, man. Jeff promised me this town, and now it's time to collect," Sal said. "He told me all about The Skulls. You rule this town. Well, now it's time to get the fuck out of here, and I'm giving you a fresh start."

Tate's lips wobbled, and tears fell from her eyes.

"What?" Murphy looked up at him.

"I'm going to let you chose. I've watched you, and I like you. Also, I like giving fuckers hard choices. So, here is the time for you to choose."

His heart raced, staring at Tate.

"Your club or your woman. Pick which one lives."

****

Tate sobbed at the ultimatum. This wasn't fair. She couldn't let him choose between her or the club.

"No, Murphy, pick the club," she said.

"Shut it, bitch." Sal pressed the knife tight against her throat.

Glancing to her left she saw her father in a pool of his own blood. Whimpering, Tate looked at the man she loved. She knew who he was going to choose, but it was the wrong one.

"No, you can't do this. The club is everything. It's not just me, Murphy, it's the whole fucking town." Tate screamed, trying to get him to realize the truth before him. This man was going to ruin everything The Skulls had built up.

"I promised you, Tate."

"No, no promise. You pick the club. Not me. I get it. I understand it, but I was too fucking stubborn to tell you."

She couldn't believe after all this time she was begging to be second place. Gazing around the room she saw them all and knew they'd be destroyed if he picked her. She saw Lash and Angel, dead before her. Eva and Tiny, a wasted love that never got chance. No, she wouldn't be responsible for what was going to happen.

Sal tightened his grip on her waist. It was uncomfortable as she stared at Murphy.

"You don't want to do this," she said.

"Pick, Murphy," Sal said. "I'm going to own this town, and your club is going down."

Staring into his eyes, Tate tried to convince him. "I love you, and I finally get what you did. I understand what you did, and you don't need to do this. I was too fucking stubborn. Forgive me." She was sobbing as she begged him.

"Your woman or the club, Murphy, pick."

"I'm not letting you down again. I pick the future." The gun Murphy had been holding behind his back was raised. One shot rang out. Tate felt a burning in her shoulder as the bullet went through her shoulder through to the man behind her.

Before she hit the floor, Murphy held her. The man behind her went down.

He covered her as another series of shots rang out. Tate felt nothing but pain, horrible, all-consuming pain through her shoulder.

Closing her eyes she heard the screaming, and then Murphy was looking down at her.

Everything felt silent. "You shot me," she said, pushing a hand to her shoulder. Her hand came away covered with blood.

"I had to choose, and I chose to keep him waiting," Murphy said.

"You think you can take my fucking town you piece of shit." The sound of her uncle's voice cut through her pain.

"Alex?"

"I saw him coming and knew I needed to stall what was happening," Murphy said.

"You shot me." Everyone was alive, and she'd been shot. Tate was so thankful Murphy had shot her.

He helped her to her feet. She looked around to see men dead on the ground. Her father was leaning against the wall looking deathly pale. Eva was pressing a towel against his stomach. Alex was beating on the man known as Sal. The drug dealer was being pummeled. Killer, Time, and Whizz were working over some men with The Lions cut.

She was starting to feel sick.

A few feet away from Tiny, she saw Mikey on the floor. He wasn't moving.

"Mikey," she said, moving over.

"Murphy, stop her," Tiny said.

"Let him go." Murphy held her tight, stopping her from going to the other man.

"No, Mikey can't be dead. He's a Skull. He can't be dead," Tate said, panicking at the lack of life in the man. She'd seen a lot of death in the last year, but nothing could have prepared her for his death.

"We need an ambulance," Eva said. "Tiny's bleeding out, and he's not going to make it if we don't do something more."

"An ambulance is on the way," Alex said.

Unable to breathe, Tate looked toward her uncle. A scream rumbled up in her chest as with one quick swipe across the neck, Alex ended the drug dealer's life.

"No one touches my niece and gets away with it."

"Tate, breathe, baby," Murphy said.

It was all too much. She couldn't breathe, and suddenly the room went black.

****

The sound of beeping woke Tate up. Opening her eyes she saw the blank white walls, and the smell of the hospital invaded all of her senses. Trying to focus on everything that happened she tried to sit up in bed only to be held back by the pain from her shoulder. Gasping, Tate felt all the memories invade.

"I'm here, honey," Tiny said.

Turning her head she saw her father in a wheelchair, wearing a hospital gown and staring at her. He held her hand, and she finally noticed the tears in his eyes. "What's going on? It all happened, didn't it? Where's Murphy and Eva?" she asked, struggling to sit up.

"If you don't stop struggling the nurse is going to shove a needle into your vein," Alex said, making his presence known. Glancing up, she saw her uncle stood by the door.

"Eva and Murphy went to get coffee and check on the damage," Alex said.

"What happened? Please, don't keep me in the dark."

"Sal is an old employee of mine. I cut him loose five years ago when I caught him stealing with intent to sell for double the price. I don't let men get away with shit like that." Alex closed the door, stepping closer. "As punishment, my men castrated him, and we believed he'd been fed to the dogs. No body was found, so I thought that was the end of it. I was wrong." Alex sat on the other side of her bed.

Tears gathered in her eyes. "He, erm, wanted revenge."

"He set his sights on Fort Wills. When Tiny told me the details I knew it was him. I got to town as soon as I could. When I saw what happened I tried to get in there as quickly as I could. He'd gotten Jeff from The Lions hooked and intended to use the club as a front, turning Fort Wills back into a dealing town. I couldn't let that happen. I promised your mother on her death bed I'd keep this town safe."

"Which is why he's moving back," Tiny said.

Glancing at her father, Tate felt the tears fall. "Tell me he didn't die."

Tiny looked down. "I'm sorry, baby, Mikey didn't make it. The bullet entered his heart, and he died instantly."

Covering her face with one hand Tate let out the sobs. Mikey was like family. He'd been part of her family for such a long time. "He shouldn't have died. Did, erm, did anyone else die?" she asked.

"Fern was shot in the head."

Tate gasped. No one liked the sweet-butt, but hearing her death still hurt.

"Sandy is in intensive care. She lost too much blood, but they're keeping an eye on her." Tate listened to them reel off the list of casualties. "Angel, erm, she lost the baby. Lash and Angel didn't even know they were expecting. She lost the baby, and they're handling it together."

"Everything that could go wrong, did," she said.

"Murphy hasn't left your side. The nurses complained about him all the time," Tiny said.

"People have died," she said.

"We're going to take care of everything." Alex looked at her father.

"What?" she asked.

"Nash found Kate's body. She was in a pool of her own vomit with a needle in her arm. We believe she sold out our location, and they used Sophia to distract us. Nothing is happening with the other woman. She's an innocent in all this," Alex said.

Murphy knocked on the door. She looked at him and smiled. Tears were running down her face, but he was the only person she wanted to see.

He carried several cups of coffee, Eva followed behind him. Within seconds he was beside her bed. "You're awake, baby." He kissed her head, and she reached toward him holding him close.

The others left her room with Tiny promising to return when visiting hours were over.

Her man lay on the bed beside her, holding her tightly in his arms. She let go of all the years and the pain inside her.

"You were going to pick me, weren't you?" she asked, thinking about that moment when he'd been given the ultimatum.

"Yes."

"I'm so pleased you didn't. I couldn't have handled their deaths, Murphy. Thank you for not picking me."

"I can't live without you, Tate. The club and all that shit I can. You, I can't get a new you. From the time when you were sixteen and adorable to your tempting self at eighteen, I was hooked on you." He kissed the top of her head. "I will always choose you."

"That's what you did when you went to The Lions, wasn't it?" she asked.

"You deserve a town to be safe. I did everything for you."

He rubbed her stomach, caressing an arm down her body.

"I don't know how we're all going to handle this," Tate said.

"They're thinking of a joint funeral for all the lives lost. Kate, Fern, and Mikey."

Tate sobbed at the mention of the older man. "He deserved so much better."

"I know."

Murphy held her until the sobbing stopped. He leaned down and kissed her head.

"Marry me," he said, producing a ring in front of her.

"What?" she asked, looking at the ring and then at him.

"I know it's not romantic. I shot you and now I'm asking for you to marry me, but I want you, Tate. Marry me."

"I've been a total bitch to you. I blamed you for everything, and it wasn't your fault at all." She shook her head, shocked by his proposal.

"I don't care. You can make it up to me."

"How?" she asked, swallowing past the lump in her throat.

"Well, I've got some kinky desires for us to play out. Also, you can be sweet to me when no one else is watching. Marry me, Tate. I don't give a fuck about anything else."

"Yes," she said, taking the ring from him and placing it on her finger. She admired the jewel on her ring finger. It was perfect.

Later that night, after Murphy left, Tiny was wheeled into her bedroom. "I didn't want you to sleep alone," he said, easing up onto her bed.

"Hey, Daddy," she said, moving over for him to fit on the bed. She turned the volume down on the bed television so she could hear him.

"No man is ever going to be good enough for you. Murphy, he did what I'd want him to do," Tiny said.

Looking up at him she saw tears in his eyes. "What do you mean?"

"I'd have chosen you. Any man who'll chose the club over you is not a man in my book. Murphy was going to choose you, and I think it's only fair he gets you back." Tiny lifted her hand in the air, staring at the engagement ring. "I gave him my blessing, and it's time you stopped being a bitch."

She chuckled. "I've already made a deal with him."

"Good."

"What are you going to do about Eva?" she asked, snuggling closer.

"I'm going to do everything I can to make it right."

They were silent for several minutes, watching the television together.

"I'm sorry about Mikey, Dad."

"Me too, pet, me, too."

MURPHY

Chapter Thirteen

The funerals were the worst part of the aftermath of the drug shooting in Fort Wills. Murphy was surprised by the turn out of the people as they put Kate, Fern, and Mikey to rest. They were all members of the club, and that made every minute of that day hard. Throughout it all, Tate was by his side, holding his hand. The engagement band lay on her finger, making everything easier for him to bear.

The club was being rebuilt, and the truck had been tipped. The bodies from the drug dealers and the few remaining Lions were buried away far out of Fort Wills. Murphy got the satisfaction of digging the graves himself. He told Tate everything, never leaving anything out. They were currently living with Tiny and Eva, back at Tiny's home. Murphy was looking for their own place, but nothing was close enough to the club.

Tate wanted to redesign his cabin. He wouldn't let her. There were too many awful memories back at the cabin, and he didn't want married life with Tate to start with them. After the funerals, morale was at an all-time low. Pictures were placed around the bar and the club of their fallen members.

Four weeks after the funeral, Tate finally broke the ice with everyone. All the members were sat at the breakfast table, including Sandy, when she clapped her hands gaining their attention.

"We're all miserable, and we've lost some great men." Her gaze went to the pictures on the wall. "But I think Mikey would want us to move on. Daddy, I want to get married inside the club," she said.

"What?" Tiny asked, spitting coffee into the cup. Murphy knew he'd been working on the cost of a church wedding for her.

"I know, it's insane right? This club is my whole life, and it's Murphy's. Also, Steven, Blaine, Killer, Whizz, and Time need to be patched in. What better way of kicking off the rest of our lives by having a huge celebration of it?" Tate asked.

The idea was horrible and required some negotiations with a priest to get him to agree, which led to Murphy staring at his reflection in the bathroom mirror next to the kitchen, two weeks later about to get married.

Killer was stood beside him. "Are you ready for this?"

Looking at his new friend, Murphy nodded. "I'm more ready than I ever thought possible."

Finishing off his tie, he turned away from the mirror to look at one of his brothers. Killer had been patched in along with the others an hour before. Tate wanted to have the rest of the night for her celebration. "Your woman knows how to start a party," Killer said, sipping from his beer.

Murphy wasn't allowed to drink until after they were man and wife.

"Tate's a good woman," he said, agreeing. Inside he was dancing for a joy at finally having her in his life. By the end of the day he was going to have her by his side and in his life with no chance of her disappearing.

"I'm seeing Kelsey," Killer said, shocking Murphy into silence.

"What? You've got to be careful. Kelsey's not part of the club."

"Neither was Angel, but look at the other two. They're stronger than ever before."

Angel had ended up in the mental ward after losing the baby. She'd completely lost it and had almost taken her own life. Lash had intervened, and now the couple were back on form. Murphy knew it was difficult for the pair of them, but slowly, they were growing stronger, healthier. He wanted to dispute that but decided to leave it. Tate would deal with Killer. He'd heard from the man himself the threat she'd given Killer. His woman had some balls, and he loved her all the more for it.

Closing his eyes, Murphy counted to ten in order to gain focus of everything that was about to happen.

"She's turned the club that's not part of the rebuild into a fucking doll's house," Nash said, storming into the room.

"Tate's only going to get married once," Murphy said. "Did Sophia turn up?" His woman had invited the other woman to try to help Sophia through her loss.

"She's on her way. Today should be good for her," Nash said, sitting on the edge of the sink. "You're going to make Tate very happy."

Murphy nodded. Next, Tiny walked through the door. The older man held a walking stick to help him get around during his recovery. Eva was by his side at the club or at the house most of the day. "You better not fuck this up, Dillon. You hurt my daughter, and I'll end you."

"Who's the big guy around Eva?" Nash asked, stopping Tiny's warning.

He sent Nash a thankful smile before focusing on Tiny and the way the man paled. "That man is Eva's father. He owns some of the underground fighting rings in Vegas and is the recent business partner with Alex."

Frowning, Murphy went to the door to see Alex and the big guy talking.

"I'm confused," he said, turning to his soon to be father-in-law. "Eva's part of some illegal fighting?"

"Her father made a lot of money in Vegas," Tiny said, looking out of the window. "She hasn't talked to him in a long time. I don't know why."

"Fuck, you're fucked," Nash said, laughing.

"Maybe you're going to know what it's like to be on the receiving end of some angry dad action," Murphy said.

Eva knocked on the door and entered. "Tate's ready for you."

All eyes turned to her.

"What?" she asked.

"You never mentioned who your father was," Tiny said.

"I didn't want to get the job for being known as Ned Walker's daughter. His reputation is known far and wide. We had a fight, and I didn't want him to know where I was. When I met Alex and knew him, I was worried he'd tell Ned where I was."

"Your father is not the leader of some biker club?" Tiny asked.

"No, he does the fighting and invests in other activities. Daddy shouldn't even be here. Alex told him about everything. I'm not involved in him being here," Eva said. "Can we not make this about me? This is Tate's day, and I don't want to ruin that with family drama that doesn't concern you."

She left the room.

"Fucking woman." Tiny turned to him. "Be at the fucking alter or I'll hunt you down."

Out of everything, Tate had been able to make an altar. She truly did amaze him.

Leaving the bathroom, Murphy left everyone alone and headed toward the altar where the priest stood waiting, holding a Bible. The man didn't look as nervous as Murphy thought he would. Being in The Skulls' zone put a lot of people off. He wondered how much cash had been thrown at the other man to make him comfortable.

Turning toward the room, he saw Lash and Angel along the front seat with Kelsey sat beside them. The entire club was sat waiting for the momentous occasion.

Eva was nowhere to be seen as she was the one and only bridesmaid. Tate had wanted Angel and Kelsey to be one, but both women didn't want to be one. It was strange as most women loved it. Kelsey was too shy, and Angel hated the limelight after everything that happened.

Simple, their wedding was going to be a simple occasion.

The music started up, and Murphy was ready to become a husband.

Tate appeared at the bottom of the stairs. She wore a white silk dress that molded to every single lush curve. There was a scar on her shoulder where the bullet had entered. She was already booked into a tattoo parlor to get it covered.

The world fell away as he looked at her. She was so fucking beautiful, and she made his world shine. For a long time he was alone, fighting everyone and everything. Then he'd entered The Skulls, been given her as a prospect duty, and his future was cemented.

His time at The Lions was worth it to live through this day. Tiny handed her over to him. He didn't feel the pain as Tiny gripped his hand tightly. Nothing else mattered other than Tate.

He'd have married her in some trashy place in Vegas so long as the marriage stuck.

"I love you," she said, mouthing the words for him to see.

When it came to the part of their vows, Tate looked nervously at him. Didn't she think he was ready?

"Tate Johnson, I promise to love, honor, and cherish you for the rest of my life. There will be no other woman in my heart or on my cock." His words got a few laughs and a growl from Tiny. "From the moment you looked at me I was lost to everything else. The best part of my day was having you in it." He didn't look away, wanting Tate to know, on this special day, how important she was to him. "Everything I've done has been for you to have a better world. Tate, my love, my life. I'm a Skull but more importantly, I'm your Skull. You'll be my first priority, you're my family, my wife, and everything I hold dear. I will die for you, kill for you, and I'll be there for you when you need it the most."

The priest cleared his throat. Glancing at their audience, he saw some of the brothers sniggering. They could snigger. He had the balls to tell his woman clearly what she meant to him.

From that day forward, Murphy was going to be in heaven.

****

"Dillon James, my Murphy, I didn't write any vows. We've come so far that I didn't think we needed any. We're stronger together than ever before. I love you more than life itself. You know I'll love, honor, and cherish you. You're the only man I've ever loved. The only man I've ever been with." Tate cut off to glare at her father. "That's right, Dad, I was a virgin."

Murphy chuckled, looking a slight shade paler.

"Life goes by so quickly. Mikey should be here, but he's not. I want to live my life to the fullest with no regrets. You're the person I want to spend my future with, grow old together, and die knowing we did everything together. I love you, and that'll never change."

The priest finished off his sermon and pronounced them man and wife.

Her man didn't wait for permission to kiss her. Murphy tugged her close and consumed her mouth with his fiery kiss. Applause, cries, and claps filled the air as she was finally given to her man. Resting her head on his shoulder, Tate gripped the fabric of his jacket. He'd agreed to the wedding she wanted.

Looking up, she saw him smiling down at her.

"You're my wife now."

It didn't take long for the priest to leave and the party to be taken outside. The club was still under a lot of building work, but it was where she wanted to get married.

After the first dance, Tiny pulled her into his arms. Her father looked nervous. She'd met Eva's father and liked Ned. He was a nice man and reminded her a little of her own father.

"I can't believe you're married," Tiny said, holding her tight.

"What are you going to do about Eva? Ned isn't the type of guy who'll take kindly to a man hurting his daughter."

She watched her father look in the other woman's direction. "She's better off without me."

"Eva loves you, Dad. Don't give up because of fear. Mom loved you, and I know she made you happy. Give love a chance. I gave a chance to Murphy, and look at me now."

"You're a beautiful bride, baby. I'd give you the whole world and hurt anyone who got in my way, you know that, right?" Tiny asked.

"I know that. It's time for you to focus on Eva. Not me. I'm going to be a wife, and I'm hoping to be a mother someday," she said, adding in the last part quietly. She really wanted to get started on getting pregnant

Tiny jerked back looking at her. She warned him to be quiet. "I'm not pregnant now, Dad."

"I'm too young to be a granddaddy, Tate. Wait for me to be ready."

She chuckled. "You're too old to be a father to a new baby, but you'll be giving Eva children when you get your head out of your ass."

"Your mother would be so proud," Tiny said, stopping their conversation.

"We've lost a lot of people to get here." She let her head rest on his chest.

"Yes, we have."

"Let's not lose anymore." Tate gave him a pointed look before finishing their dance. "Is everything ready?" she asked.

"Yeah, you and Murphy can leave when you're ready."

Smiling, Tate kissed her father and searched for Murphy. She found him talking with Lash and Nash. The two men were like brothers to her.

"There's the bride herself. How are you feeling?" Lash asked.

"I'm good. Are you ready to go?" she asked her husband. It would take her some time to get used to that.

"You want to leave?" he asked.

"I've got something I want to show you."

They said their goodbyes, and the club waved them off. Murphy drove a car instead of a bike with the "Just Married" sign on the back.

"Take me to your cabin," she said.

"Tate, we don't have to go to the cabin," he said.

"Just do as I ask."

She leaned against his shoulder as he drove all the way to his cabin. He parked the car, and Tate climbed out, picking up her wedding dress as they moved toward the front door.

"I hate this place," Murphy said, slamming the door to the car closed.

"No, you don't. You'll see the good once I'm done." Taking his hand, she led him up the stairs toward the front door. Extracting the key from under the plant pot, Tate opened the front door.

"I didn't leave a key there," he said.

"No, I did. Stop getting paranoid." Leading the way into his house she made him stop at the front room. She'd started redecorating two weeks ago. Her father made sure Murphy didn't come near the cabin. "What do you think?"

"You're decorating."

Shaking her head, she tugged him into the room. "You own this cabin. I remember you talking about it with fondness. Yes, there are bad memories because of your times with The Lions, but I don't want you to give it up."

Pulling the pin from her hair, Tate started to get unclothed.

"Tate, what are you doing?" he asked.

"It's time to make new memories. This is where we're going to live. You're going to build a good fence around the lake so our kids cannot drown, and together you and I are going to bring this cabin back to its former glory." Tate pushed him into the nearest chair and straddled his legs.

Reaching behind her, she tugged at the zipper. Murphy finished pulling the zipper down, and she pushed the dress from her body exposing her breasts.

She heard him hiss seconds before thumbing the nipples.

"Is this part of your strategy to get me liking the cabin?" he asked.

"Yes, is it working?"

"A little. You're going to have to work really hard."

Kissing his lips, Tate worked his mouth, going down his neck to nibble on the flesh of his earlobe.

"Murphy?"

"Yeah."

"I really want to get pregnant. I want to have your baby."

He froze beneath her.

"You want to get pregnant?"

Leaning back she smiled down at him, cupping his face. "Yes, I want to get pregnant, and I think we're going to be good parents to our children."

His hands sank into her hair and pulled her down against him. "Fuck, woman, how can I hate this place now? I want us to be parents."

Kissing his lips, Tate worked the buckle of his belt open. Murphy helped her, easing his pants down and pulling her panties aside. He found her wetness and sank deep inside her. Tate moaned, loving the feel of his hard cock in her pussy.

"I love you, Tate," he said.

"I love you, too, Dillon."

There wasn't any need for more words. They had each other, and their future was looking better than ever before. Tate hoped they wouldn't have to deal with another man aiming a gun at her. If another man tried that shit, she was seriously going to kick some ass before her man finished them off.

Epilogue

"That's the last box," Nash said, placing it on top of the others inside Sophia's new apartment. He'd offered to help her out of the old place as he'd lost count of the number of times he'd found her sobbing. Kate had shared their old apartment, paying half the rent. He'd worked his ass off to find this place. It was more than Sophia could afford on her waitressing salary. He was the one paying for the apartment.

She had college and other things to deal with. The least he could do was pay for her place.

"Thank you, Edward." She lifted the box and dropped it on the floor. The last couple of weeks had been hard on her. He saw signs of her losing weight, and he hated it. What did someone do to help another with their grieving?

When his and Lash's parents were killed he had Lash to help him deal. Sophia didn't have anyone.

"Kate wouldn't want you to be like this," he said, following her inside the new apartment. The place was mostly bare. He'd ordered a sofa to be delivered along with anything she'd need to get by. There was no way he was leaving her alone.

She walked into a bedroom where he'd carried the single bed to. He couldn't believe she was sleeping on a single bed.

The box went on the floor. "I'm dealing with it, Edward. I'm trying. Kate was a lot of things, but she was still my sister. She loved me."

He wasn't going to hurt her by disagreeing. Kate was a nasty piece of work when she started. The first time he'd met Sophia, Kate bullied her over her weight. When they were alone, Nash recalled slamming Kate against the wall and threatening her life if she ever spoke shit like that to Sophia again.

Kate rarely talked about her little sister after that. He knew that Kate was aware of his attraction to Sophia. Still, he used Kate when the mood took him, and that was his reason for feeling guilty about the whole sorry situation.

She started to cry, and Nash couldn't handle that. Going to her side, he pulled her into his arms. Her lemony scent clawed at him to push her to the bed and force all memory of Kate from her mind. She'd be a dream to fuck.

Just another fucking thing to hate about myself.

He wanted to fuck Sophia badly. His cock was already thickening, anticipating the feel of her wrapped around his dick. She'd be so fucking tight. Sophia wasn't a virgin. He knew it because Kate loved telling him all about the asshole who broke Sophia's heart. Kate had stopped laughing when he'd told her he would kill the motherfucker for touching her.

After fucking Kate senseless, he'd found the prick and killed him, slowly. Zero had his back and helped him get rid of the body. No one would miss the prick.

Stroking her hair, Nash forced himself to focus on Sophia and her pain.

"I can't stop thinking about her. She didn't deserve to die."

"Baby, she was a druggie and almost got you killed because of it."

She pulled back and stared at him. "Don't say stuff like that, Edward. She's dead, and we don't know what happened."

He gazed down at her full, heart-shaped lips. They were so plump, wet, and inviting. Fuck, he wanted a taste. Just one little taste. Leaning close, he brushed his lips across hers. The first touch was light, and he heard her gasp. He couldn't stop as he deepened the kiss, sinking his fingers into her hair.

Nash lost complete control, plunging his tongue into her mouth, moaning as her fingers bit into his arms. He wanted her marks all over his body.

Sophia wrapped her arms around his neck, holding him close. She met his tongue with her own, and he was in bliss at the feel of her womanly curves against him.

All too soon she tore away from him.

"No, I can't do this." She took a step away, facing away from him.

"Sophia, you've got nothing to be afraid of," he said. "I want this as well."

Her teary gaze met his. "Kate was in love with you. You were with my sister. I can't do this. She would tell me in detail everything that happened to you. We're not going to be together, Edward."

"Your sister is gone."

"She'll never be gone." He watched as she grabbed a box and walked toward him. "I'm sorry if I gave you the wrong impression, but Kate will always be here and I can't love the men she did. I'm sorry, Edward. I'm not what you're looking for."

Taking the box from her arms, Nash felt his world shatter around him. The one and only woman he'd ever felt anything for and she was pushing him out of the door. "I'll, erm, come and check on you in a few weeks," he said.

"Don't bother, Edward. There's nothing for you here."

Sophia closed the door behind him.

The drive back to the club was a blur. Nash didn't see anything as he drove home. The club, The Skulls was his home. He didn't have a spare place like his brother. Charging through the doors he ignored everyone as he passed. After Sophia's rejection he needed some alone time.

Going to his room, he dropped the box on the floor and froze. He recognized Kate's jewelry box. She'd shown it to him one night when he'd gone home with her. Opening up the box, Nash saw the evidence of Kate's addiction. He'd never cared enough about Kate to see what was going on. Looking at the white powder in the bag, her addiction was glaring at him in the face.

Did he drive Kate to using?

Rolling the bag over in his hands, Nash tried to think what to do with it.

A knock at the door had him hiding the tiny white bag behind his back. His brother looked around the door.

"Hey," Lash said.

"Hey."

He felt hot and sweaty all over. What was he supposed to do with the bag?

"Angel and I are staying for dinner. I think Tate's bringing Murphy back to the club. They've got some news to give to the club. Are you going to join us?" Lash asked.

"Yeah, I'll be down in a minute," Nash said, smiling at his brother.

"Are you all right?"

"Yeah, I'm fine."

"You'd talk to me if anything was bothering you, wouldn't you?" Lash asked.

This was his chance to show the bag.

"Yeah, of course." The bag stayed behind his back.

Lash nodded. "See you downstairs."

The door shut, leaving Nash alone with the drugs. Staring at the bag, Nash wondered what it would be like to get rid of all of his troubles.

No drugs. Tiny won't allow it. Fuck over my life.

Even as he was fighting with himself to stop, Nash found himself opening the bag. Some oblivion wouldn't hurt. It was only going to be this one time.

The End

www.samcrescent.wordpress.com

Evernight Publishing

www.evernightpublishing.com